Ghost Buddy

HENRY WINKLER is known worldwide for his role as the Fonz on the series *Happy Days*. He is also an award-winning producer and director of family and children's programming, and the author (with Lin Oliver) of the Hank Zipzer series (Walker Books). Henry is a passionate advocate for child literacy in the UK and in 2011 was awarded an OBE. He lives in Los Angeles, California.

LIN OLIVER is a television producer and writer, who co-authored (with Henry Winkler) the *New York Times* bestselling Hank Zipzer series as well as many of her own titles. Lin lives in Los Angeles, California.

Henry Winkler & Lin Oliver

Ghost Buddy

Always Dance With a Buffalo

■SCHOLASTIC

To Indya Belle and Ace, who light up the world.
And to Stacey, always—H.W.

For Leo Pasquale Confalone, darling baby boy.—L.O.

Scholastic Children's Books
An imprint of Scholastic Ltd
Euston House, 24 Eversholt Street
London, nw1 1db, UK
Registered office: Westfield Road, Southam, Warwickshire, cv47 0ra
SCHOLASTIC and associated logos are trademarks and/or
registered trademarks of Scholastic Inc.

First published in the US by Scholastic Inc., 2013
First published in the UK by Scholastic Ltd., 2014

Text © Henry Winkler and Lin Oliver, 2013
Cover art © Tony Ross, 2014

The right of Henry Winkler and Lin Oliver to be identified as the
authors of this work has been asserted by them.

ishn 978 1 407 13231 0

A CIP catalogue record for this book
is available from the British Library.

Printed and bound by CPI Group (UK) Ltd, Croydon, cr0 4yy

Papers used by Scholastic Children's Books are made
from wood grown in sustainable forests.

1 3 5 7 9 10 8 6 4 2

This is a work of fiction. Names, characters, places, incidents and dialogues are
products of the author's imagination or are used fictitiously. Any resemblance
to actual people, living or dead, events of locals is entirely coincidental.

www.scholastic.co.uk/zone

Chapter 1

"I have two left feet," Billy Broccoli announced at the dinner table one rainy March evening.

"Don't leave out your twelve thumbs and six pair of eyes," his stepsister, Breeze, said, laughing so hard she nearly spit a wad of mashed potatoes back on to her plate.

"I'm not trying to be funny, Breeze," Billy complained. "This is a serious problem, and I'd appreciate a little understanding."

Billy's stepfather, Bennett Fielding, put down his fork and placed one elbow on the kitchen table. Billy knew what was coming. This was Bennett's typical pose when he was about to go off on a long, boring explanation, usually involving teeth or some aspect of dental health. He was a very devoted dentist.

"Scientifically speaking," Dr Fielding began, "the odds of any human having two left feet are extremely rare. But then, nature is full of amazing surprises. For instance, take your lowly snail. Its mouth is no larger than the head of a pin, yet snails can have up to twenty-five-thousand teeth."

"And that fits into this conversation exactly how, Dad?" Breeze asked.

"I'm just saying, Breezy, that if Billy actually did have two left feet, it would be worthy of going into the *Guinness Book of World Records*."

Billy's mother, Charlotte Broccoli-Fielding, poured herself another glass of lemonade from the pitcher on the table. She was known for making some of the best lemonade in all of Los Angeles. Being the head teacher of Billy and Breeze's middle school, she was also known for understanding what middle schoolers were trying to say even when they weren't saying it very well.

"I think what Billy means, Bennett, is that he has trouble dancing," she explained.

"Exactly, Mum!" Billy shouted, relieved that someone finally understood what his actual problem was. "When I try to dance, it's like my feet go in opposite directions. One goes to Oregon. The other goes to Argentina."

"As long as your feet stop stinking up the house, I don't care where they go," Breeze muttered.

"For your information," Billy said, a little offended, "my feet do not smell. I make it a habit to change my socks at least once a week. And if I don't, I'm careful to place my socks by an open window to air out overnight."

Breeze made a gagging sound. "Eeuuuww," was the only syllable she could utter.

"Maybe it's time you changed your socks every day, honey," Mrs Broccoli-Fielding suggested gently, putting a supportive hand on

3

Billy's arm. "When you become a tween, you have to step up your grooming a notch."

"Or in his case, twenty notches," Breeze added.

"People, this is not helping me with my problem." Billy pushed his half eaten meatballs and mashed potatoes away, to emphasize the point that he was trying to have a serious conversation. "I have to learn a traditional Native American dance by the end of the week, and I can't do it. As I was saying before I was so rudely interrupted by a certain thirteen-year-old named Breeze Fielding, I have two left feet."

"Is it a complicated dance?" Mrs Broccoli-Fielding asked.

"It is for me. I can't remember what comes after what."

"I have a suggestion," Bennett said. "You could put down individual pieces of paper on the rug and use them to create a chart of where your feet should go. It's like reading for your feet."

He sat back in his chair and smiled, very pleased with himself for coming up with this great idea. Bennett often came up with unique solutions to problems, like when he decided to use his mobile phone case clipped on his belt to hold his dental floss. He proudly demonstrated that little invention to all his dental patients for weeks afterwards. Billy felt bad about having to burst his bubble on his "reading for feet" concept.

"Making that chart would take for ever, Bennett, and I have to know this dance soon. We're demonstrating how the Chumash tribe celebrated, and our dance has to be perfect by Friday night."

"Oh, now I understand," Billy's mum said. "You're performing for the Native American Night celebration at the Natural History Museum." Noticing the puzzled look on Bennett's face, she added, "Every year, our school does a unit on Native American culture, and the final performance is at the museum.

The teachers tell me that this year, all the parents are attending. We're expecting a big crowd."

Billy's stomach did a flip flop that had nothing to do with the meatballs or the mashed potatoes. It was sheer, raw nervousness.

"You're making it worse, Mum," he said. "Thinking about all those people watching me makes me absolutely one hundred per cent sure I'm going to totally mess up."

"Nonsense. You'll be great, honey. Everything you do is great."

"Oh yeah?" Billy got up from the table and started to pace around the kitchen. "That's not what Ruby Baker said. She's my partner and she said I was stepping all over her feet. Today she was wearing trainers, but on Friday, she'll be wearing moccasins. One mistake and I could crush her big toe. And all the little ones, too."

"What you need is a private dance instructor," Breeze said, gathering the plates from the table. "Someone cool, a great dancer, who can really show you the moves."

"Did someone call?" said a ghostly voice from the kitchen doorway. "I happen to be the move master. When I glide across the dance floor, I've literally seen women faint."

It was Hoover Porterhouse the Third, who had just come in from his evening float around the neighbourhood. Of course, he was only visible to Billy, as he was Billy's personal ghost. But like all ghosts, Hoover left a trail of cold air wherever he went. Breeze shivered.

"Billy," she said, zipping up her hoodie. "Don't you think it's weird that half the time I'm around you, I'm freezing cold? Are you a ghost or something?"

Billy forced himself to laugh, much too loud and much too long for the situation.

"A ghost?" he roared, almost choking on his words. "Are you crazy, Breeze? There's no such thing as ghosts!"

"You don't have to laugh like a wild hyena, Billy. It's creepy. Besides, some people believe in ghosts."

"Like me, for instance," the Hoove said, floating over next to Breeze and whispering in her ear. "I'm a big believer."

Billy wondered if perhaps Breeze was catching on to Hoover's presence in their house. It had been three months since the day they moved in and Billy first discovered that a fourteen-year-old ghost had been living in his bedroom wardrobe for the last ninety-nine years. Could it be that so many close encounters with the Hoove was making Breeze suspicious? Could she have figured out Billy's secret? Why else would she make a random ghost comment?

Bennett leaned in, cleared his throat and put his elbow on the table for the second time.

"Uh-oh," Breeze whispered to Billy. "Here comes another science lecture."

"You started it," Billy whispered back. "You and your ghost talk."

Bennett had already launched into a long-winded explanation of what might account for people believing in ghosts.

"Sometimes, people hear a strange sound and can't identify where it's coming from, or observe an unusual phenomenon that doesn't present a clear explanation," he droned. "So they wrongly assume it's a ghostly presence."

The Hoove let out a rip-roaring belly laugh.

"Oh yeah! Wrongly assume this presence!" he howled.

He hovered next to the kitchen table and knocked a fork, knife and spoon off the table. As they clattered to the floor, both Breeze and Billy's mum let out a startled gasp.

"And here we have a perfect example of what I was talking about," Bennett continued without missing a beat.

"Are you saying we have a ghost in our kitchen at this very moment?" Breeze asked.

"Exactly the opposite. Billy simply knocked some silverware off the table and it made a noise. No reason to assume we have a ghost."

"Except that you do have one," Hoover

sniggered, reaching up to turn his tartan newsboy cap backwards with a confident air. "And, I might add, a perfect specimen of a ghost at that."

"You wish," Billy whispered to him.

"No I don't," Breeze answered, thinking Billy was talking to her. "I don't wish for ghosts. I wish for important things like a new pair of black boots or world peace. Stuff like that."

The Hoove had grown impatient with the conversation of his non-existence. He was real. He knew it and Billy knew it, so to him, this was wasting his time.

"Come on, Billy Boy," he said, tapping him on the shoulder. "You want to learn to dance or not? I'll meet you in your room and show you some moves. That is, if you can break away from all this dinner-table fun and games."

The Hoove drifted off down the hall towards Billy's room. Billy picked up his dinner and salad plate and took them over to the kitchen counter.

"May I be excused?" he said as he carefully stacked them in the dishwasher.

"Why? Did you cut the cheese again?" Breeze asked.

"That's so funny I forgot to laugh," Billy answered. "I'll be in my room, and I'd prefer not to be disturbed. I have a lot of dance steps to learn."

"You do that," Breeze said. "I can't wait to see what you do with the Chumash Cha-Cha."

By the time Billy got to his room, the Hoove had pushed all the furniture to the edges of the walls and tossed Billy's dirty clothes into the wardrobe.

"I have created a dance floor for our lesson," he announced. "Every great performer needs a stage. Close the door, Billy Boy. Make yourself comfortable and observe."

Billy perched on the edge of his bed while the Hoove placed himself smack in the middle of the room. He pulled his tartan cap down over his left eye, snapped his suspenders, and assumed a very theatrical position.

"The key to dancing is all in the sway," he began, barely rocking his transparent body to and fro. "Never mind all those made-up steps everyone does. They ruin the mood."

"But Hoove, the Chumash dances have a lot of steps. Very detailed steps, as a matter of fact. And swaying is not one of them."

"The trouble with you, Billy Boy, is that you follow the crowd. Remember the Hoove's Rule Number Five. Never be afraid to do what your smooth self tells you to do."

The Hoove floated around the made-up dance floor, turning and dipping and swaying to whatever music was in his head.

"Toss me your baseball bat," he said to Billy as he swept by him.

"Why, are you going to dance your way to first base?"

"I need a partner," the Hoove said. "And

in the absence of a great-looking girl, I will demonstrate with this stick of wood."

Billy picked up one of the wooden bats that was leaning against the wall and threw it to the Hoove, who snatched it out of the air and held it close to him. To Billy, it looked like the Hoove was dancing with the bat. But to anyone else, it would have looked like the bat was spinning on its own in mid-air.

"The important thing," the Hoove pointed out as he two-stepped around the room, "is to move in time with the music."

"So Hoove, can I just point out one little thing? There is no music."

"Don't get your undies in a bundle over details. And while you're at it, toss me that other bat."

Billy did, and once again, the Hoove caught it in mid-air. Then he picked up Billy's metal wastebasket and put it on top of the desk. Using the bats as drumsticks and the wastebasket as a drum, he started to beat out a rhythm.

"You want music, there's your music," he said. "It's your basic turkey trot, a classic beat in the dance world."

"Well, I hate to burst your bubble, Hoove, but the Chumash weren't exactly turkey trotters. They danced to pay respect to their ancestors. And to thank Mother Earth for the harvest and the Heavens for the rain. It had nothing to do with turkeys or trotting. It looked more like this."

Billy hunched down low to the ground and started to twirl in a small circle, hopping on one foot and then the other. Just as he was starting to get into the rhythm, though, his feet got tangled up into a ball and he fell over on to the rug.

"You see?" Billy moaned. "There's the proof. I can't do this."

"You have to practise. I'll drum and you do it again. And this time, don't bend over so far. Your butt is sticking out so far it looks like a landing platform for a helicopter."

Settling himself down on the top of the desk, the Hoove pounded out a rhythm on the wastebasket. Billy hunched down and started to circle again, this time letting out a loud whoop as he spun round and round. The clatter of the drums combined with Billy's whoops attracted the spying eye of Rod Brownstone, Billy's next-door neighbour. He sneaked out of his room and crept along the gravel path between their two houses until he came to the window that looked into Billy's room. Pressing his face up against the glass, Brownstone saw Billy dancing in a circle and two bats floating in mid-air. His jaw practically came unhinged and dropped to the window sill.

"I knew it," he whispered to himself. "Weird things happen inside this house."

Reaching down to his belt, he grabbed the walkie-talkie that he kept clipped there in case of emergency. As far as Rod Brownstone was concerned, no emergency was too small. He held the walkie-talkie up close to his mouth.

"Dad," he whispered. "Come in, Dad. Emergency situation existing at 632 Fairview. Over."

There was static on the other end, and then Rod's father's voice could be heard.

"What is it this time, son?"

"Deputy Brownstone reporting two floating bats that are assaulting a wastebasket. I need you here to make an arrest."

"Arrest who, Rod? A baseball bat?"

"Just get here, Dad. Over and out."

Rod Brownstone continued to press his face against the window, watching Billy and the Hoove practise the dance. Just as Rod heard his father's footsteps on the gravel path, Billy collapsed on the floor inside his room, panting for air.

"I can't breathe," he gasped. "Those Chumash must have been in great shape. I wonder if they had treadmills back then."

"Dad, hurry!" Brownstone whispered into the walkie-talkie. "You're going to miss it."

Inside, Billy had crawled over to his bed and flopped down, clutching his sides.

"That was harder than the push-ups we do at baseball practice," he said to the Hoove.

The Hoove put down the bats and floated over to Billy.

"I got to be honest with you, Billy Boy. The dance is not looking good. In fact, it's looking extremely weak. I hate to break it to you, pal, but no crops are growing because of your dancing."

"But I didn't fall down this last time. That's an improvement, isn't it?"

"Dancing requires more than staying on your feet. You got to look good, feel the passion, and know the moves. Which means you're going need some intensive help."

"What does that mean, exactly?"

"That means I am taking the bull by the horns and coming to your school tomorrow. I will be there when you practise with Ruby, to guide your feet and show you the rhythmic way to success. It's going to be Hoove-tastic."

"Does it make any difference at all that I don't want you at my school?"

"Not even a drop. Face it, you need me, Billy Boy. I'll come to your rehearsal, learn the steps . . . instantaneously, I might add . . . give them my unique flair, and finally will pass them on to you, you lucky ducky."

Billy put his face in his hands and moaned.

"Just let me rest for a minute, OK? Then we can try again."

"Have it your way. I'll be relaxing in your wardrobe. We will begin Round Two of instruction after you've recovered."

The Hoove drifted across the room and floated through the door of Billy's wardrobe, stretching out along the top shelf that used to contain Billy's jumpers and shoes. Outside, Rod's father had arrived at the window.

"All right, son, where's the perpetrator?"

"In there, Dad," Rod said, pointing into Billy's room. "Talking to himself."

Mr Brownstone looked in the window, and then frowned at his son.

"All I see is a kid lying on his bed. The worst thing he's doing is covering his face in his hands, which is not at all illegal."

Rod looked in. He saw Billy on his bed, the bats lying on the desk top, unmoving.

"You've done it again, Rod." His father shook his head. "You've taken me away from my favourite TV show and got me out here for nothing."

"But those bats were floating, Dad. I swear it. Just wait two more minutes, and you'll see it happen again. I promise."

Mr Brownstone made an irritated clicking sound with his tongue.

"Give me that walkie-talkie," he said, snatching it from Rod's hands. "I forbid you to use an intelligence device until you know how to use it properly. And that does not involve making up ridiculous stories and spying on good neighbours who are just going about their business."

Taking Rod by the collar, he guided him firmly away from the window and back to their house. Poor Rod Brownstone had to spend the rest of the evening in his room, writing a paragraph on "Why I Will Not Treat Police Equipment as a Toy and Waste My Father's Time Again". As his pencil moved across the paper, Rod Brownstone couldn't possibly know that across the garden, the baseball bats were at it again.

But this time, they were doing the turkey trot.

Chapter 2

The next morning, Billy was awakened to the sound of things being thrown around in his wardrobe. When he opened his eyes, he saw his baseball hats flying out of the wardrobe door and landing on the rug in the middle of the room.

"Hey, those are my hats," he grumbled, rubbing the sleep out of his eyes. "Leave them alone."

"I'm looking for your Dodgers hat," the Hoove shouted from inside the wardrobe. "And by the way, you should really get your stuff organized in here. This is an embarrassment. Normal people do not keep their tighty whities on hangers."

"Normal people do not have ghosts in their wardrobe telling them what to do before they've even opened their eyes. And besides, why do you need my Dodgers hat?"

"I'm going to school today, remember. I want to blend in with you modern guys."

"Trust me, Hoove. Floating hats do not blend in. Just the opposite. They freak people out."

"Got it!" the Hoove called out, and before Billy could even pull back the covers, he saw his blue-and-white Dodger baseball hat float out of the wardrobe.

"How does it look on me?" the Hoove asked.

"I can't see you. All I can see is the bill of the hat bobbing up and down and it's making me seasick."

The Hoove started to whistle "I've Been Working on the Railroad", which usually made him materialize. As he got into the song, parts of his body began to appear. First a leg, then a neck, then a belly button.

"Hoove, concentrate," Billy said. "You're only partly there. And not your best parts, either."

"I'm trying," the Hoove snapped. "My whistling isn't too sharp today."

"Well, try harder. Because no matter how many months we've been together, I still can't get used to seeing your belly button floating around my room."

The Hoove put his mind to it, and threw his whistling into hyper breath, finishing the song in record time. His concentration paid off, and by the end of the song, he had materialized and stood before Billy fully formed with a Dodger hat perched on his wavy black hair.

"I'm dressed," he said. "Now it's your turn. Hurry up and let's get out of here. Moorepark Middle School – you better be ready, because here I come."

"Hoove, you have to promise me you're not going to make a scene at school."

"I never *try* to make a scene, but when you have my special gift, people gather. They can't help themselves."

"Fine, then you're not coming unless you swear to me that you'll keep a low profile."

"Billy Boy. I'm going to be so low that I could walk under a sofa with my hat on."

Billy snatched the Dodger cap off the Hoove's head.

"No hats, no sofas, no commotion, no trouble," he said in a stern tone of voice. "Deal?"

The Hoove just laughed.

"When was the last time you can recall me making trouble for you?"

"Hoove, no discussion. Just say deal and let's go."

"All right. Here it comes! Deal. And by the way, you might want to change out of your pyjamas before you set out for school. I'm just suggesting."

After breakfast, Billy put his homework in his rucksack, tucked his lunch into the zip pouch, and headed out of the door.

"Hey, where's my lunch?" the Hoove called. "I can't believe that you neglected to pack me even so much as a roast beef sandwich with spicy horseradish sauce."

"You don't eat, remember?"

"So true. But it's the thought that counts."

Billy shook his head. The Hoove was in an impossible mood, so instead of responding, Billy left the house and headed down Fairview to Fulton Avenue, which was only one street away from school. As he approached the corner, he saw Ruby Baker waiting for the light to change. She was carrying a white plastic bag that was almost as big as she was. Billy picked up his pace a little to catch up to her. Walking to school with Ruby was always a great way to start the day, even if talking to girls did make him nervous.

Before he reached her, he felt a cold blast of air sweep up behind him. It was definitely a Hoove move.

"I see somebody's walking fast," the Hoove said. "What's the rush?" Then he noticed Ruby waiting at the corner. "Ohhhh," he said. "It all becomes clear."

"I don't have the slightest idea what you're talking about, Hoove."

"I'm talking about the butterflies that are setting up home in your tummy, Billy Boy. I see the way you look at her. So let me give you a very important tip you can take with you into the future. You, in particular, should never be yourself when you're trying to impress a girl. You've got to maintain your mysterious flair at all costs."

"Hoove, I'm already nervous about talking to Ruby. And you're not helping."

"Most people would pay money for my advice. Not to brag, but I have a black belt in the essence of charm."

"Oh no, she's looking over here," Billy said. "Yikes, now she's waving."

"Excellent," the Hoove answered. "And do not wave back. You never want to let the ladies know you're interested. And do not ... I repeat ... do not ever say yikes."

But it was too late. Billy's hand had already

shot into the air and was waving like a flag in the wind.

"What did I just say? Are my words invisible, too? Hoove's Rule Number 66. You never want to appear too eager."

"But I like her, Hoove."

"You can't let her know that. Don't ask me why, even the Hoove doesn't have the answer to that one. I just know that if you show too much interest, people run the other way."

"That's crazy," Billy said.

"You're telling me."

"You know what's even crazier?"

"What?"

"Ruby is walking over to me right now."

"OK, now's your moment, Broccoli. Drop your shoulders. Tilt your head. No, not like that. It looks like you're looking at her sideways. Now smile. No, not so wide. Too many teeth. You look like a wild-eyed beaver."

"Hoove, please. Could you get lost? Disappear. Like now!"

"All right, but I'm warning you. You're going to regret refusing my help."

"Go. Now."

"OK, here I go. This is me going. See you around the halls."

The Hoove switched himself into hyperglide and sped off, just as Ruby reached Billy.

"Hi, Billy," she said to him, a big smile spreading across her face.

"Uhhh . . . ummmm . . . hi," he stammered.

Ruby shifted the big bag uncomfortably in her hands.

"Can I help you with that?" Billy offered.

"That's really nice of you," Ruby said. "It's the Chumash basket we started making in art class yesterday. I took it home to work on it."

Billy reached for the bag and slung it over his shoulder, trying to look casual. It wasn't a heavy bag, but it had just enough weight to throw him off balance. He stumbled awkwardly and his rucksack slid off his shoulder and fell to the ground. Some pencils slipped out of the zip pouch and rolled down the pavement.

"Oops," Billy said, feeling like a total clod. "Hey, you runaway pencils, did I say you could roll for a walk?"

Ruby giggled and Billy was relieved that she wasn't judging him. He picked up the pencils, put them in his rucksack, and slung the plastic bag over his shoulder again, trying to maintain his balance this time.

"You know, that's a big bag," Ruby said. "Why don't we each grab a handle and carry it together."

"Great idea," Billy answered. He slid it off his shoulder, took one handle, and gave Ruby the other. It was a perfect arrangement.

The light changed to green and they stepped off the kerb together. They were silent until they reached the other side of the street. Billy searched for something to say.

"I'm glad to see you can still walk," he said finally. "I'm sorry I crunched your toes yesterday during the Chumash dance rehearsal."

"It didn't hurt that much. You landed mostly on the rubber part of my trainers."

Billy let out a big laugh, but then, remembering the Hoove's advice about not showing too many teeth, quickly assumed a more serious expression and changed the subject.

"I bet you wish you didn't get assigned me as a partner," he said. "I have two left feet, you know. Apparently, two left thumbs also. The art teacher said my basket weaving needed big-time help. It's almost as bad as my dancing."

"Well, it probably took the Chumash kids a lot of time to learn all that stuff, too."

"Yeah, but they didn't have a performance at the museum in front of all the parents Friday night."

"Don't worry, Billy. We'll get there. It just takes practice."

"Thanks, Ruby. That's a really nice thing to say."

She gave him a big smile and he grinned back, this time not worrying about how many teeth he was showing.

In less than a minute, they reached the front of the school, a grassy area with a tall flagpole in the centre. Billy thought he heard someone shouting his name, but it sounded like it was coming from above. He looked up, and hanging off the top of the flagpole was Hoover Porterhouse the Third. He flashed Billy two big thumbs up.

"Didn't I tell you?" he called out. "You follow my advice, it works out perfectly with the ladies every time."

Billy just ignored the Hoove as he and Ruby went through the front doors and headed down the hall to class.

It was an all-Chumash morning. After form room, Billy and Ruby went to Mr Wallwetter's first period English class. Instead of doing the unit on semicolons, Mr Wallwetter announced that the class period would be devoted to a rehearsal of their Chumash dance. That was because Louise Niles, the physical education teacher, was available that period to provide special help to those having trouble with the dance steps.

"Most of you are coming along just fine," Mr Wallwetter said. "But some of you are foot challenged."

Billy felt that everyone in the class had turned their heads to look directly at him. The only thing Billy could think to do was to stare down at the floor and count to ten until that horrible moment had passed.

Mr Wallwetter divided the class into two groups. Those who needed special dance coaching stayed inside the classroom. Those who had already mastered the steps were sent down to the art room to work on their Chumash baskets. Billy took some special pleasure in noting that Rod Brownstone was also put into the group of kids with feet that refused to follow directions.

Ms Niles stood at the front of the room and demonstrated the steps slowly so that everyone could see the moves. As the kids practised, she went to each couple to work on their individual problems. Billy was having so much trouble that Ms Niles suggested he practise with a chair before trying it again with Ruby. That was all Rod Brownstone needed to hear.

"A chair!" he hooted. "Is that the only partner you could get, Broccoli? Aw, look at that. The plastic seat is falling in love with you."

"I suggest you concentrate on your own feet, which are none too graceful," Ms Niles said to him. "And remember that teasing was not the Chumash way."

Ruby could see that Billy was embarrassed.

"Billy doesn't have to practise with a chair," she said to Ms Niles. "I wore hiking boots with steel-tipped toes today as added protection."

"That was very considerate of you," Ms Niles said.

Ruby suggested that she and Billy continue to

rehearse in a corner of the room where Rod
Brownstone couldn't see them.

"Just ignore him," she said to Billy.

"I'm sorry to be such a clod," Billy said to her.
"This is so embarrassing. I'm just not good at
dancing."

He felt his face grow bright red from his
admission. He hadn't meant to be so honest –
after all, the Hoove had told him that total
honesty doesn't work with girls – but the words
just came out before he could stop himself.

"That's OK," Ruby said. "I'll bet you're good
at a lot of other things."

"So you don't think I'm a total dork?"

"No, I'm glad you're my partner. We're having
a good time. Besides, when we finally get this
dance, we'll fit right in with the Chumash."

Billy concentrated hard on the steps, counting
out loud and never taking his eyes off his feet.
He was so deep in concentration that it startled
him to hear Rod Brownstone suddenly squeal
like a pinched pig.

"Hey, who gave me that wedgie?" he called out.

Everyone in class stopped dancing and cracked up as Rod tried to secretly settle his underpants back where they belonged. Billy looked over and saw the Hoove, circling Rod, a big smile on his ghostly face.

"Just a little reminder that my assistance is not far away, Mr I-Don't-Need-Your-Help," the Hoove shouted to Billy. And then in a flash, he was gone.

Billy was so grateful when the dancing lesson was over. That is, until he realized that after dancing came Chumash basket weaving. Mr Wallwetter walked all the dancers to the art room to join the other members of the class working on their baskets. The tables were filled with basket-weaving supplies. Long strands of straw covered the tabletops, where kids were hunched over making coils and tying them together with twine.

"I am leaving you in the capable hands of Mrs

Penny," Mr Wallwetter said. "She is a parent volunteer who has graciously provided you with all of your supplies. I'm sure we're all grateful to her."

"What for?" Rod Brownstone muttered. "All she did was bring in a bunch of weeds."

"I think that perhaps the art of the Chumash basket is lost on you," Mr Wallwetter said to Rod. "Why don't you come with me on to the playground, where we have another Chumash activity that might be more suited to your . . . shall we say . . . assertive personality."

"Lead the way," Rod said, beaming proudly. He wasn't aware that Mr Wallwetter hadn't exactly given him a compliment. "People who guard the public safety like I do have to be assertive."

Rod followed Mr Wallwetter out of the room, and as he passed Billy, he muttered, "See you later, Princess Broccoli Basket."

Relieved that Rod was out of the room, Billy went to the table by the window, as far away from Mrs Penny as he could get. He knew that as bad as his feet were at dancing, his fingers were even worse at basket weaving. Billy spread his basket-making supplies all around him on the project table. He had been assigned to make a Chumash acorn tray, but the truth was, he wouldn't know an acorn tray from a twelve-legged octopus.

As he took his seat, he felt a cold rush of air next to him and smelled the tangy aroma of orange juice. Whenever the Hoove smelled like orange juice, it meant he was either upset or excited. Whichever one he was, Billy didn't want to know about it, but the Hoove gave him no choice.

"Billy," he said, tugging on Billy's sleeve. "I just saw the most outstanding sight these gorgeous eyes of mine have ever beheld. Come look."

"Not now, Hoove," Billy whispered, keeping his head down to make sure no one saw him talking. The last thing he wanted was for his classmates to think he was crazy enough to be talking to himself.

"Billy Boy, I'm begging you. Get your hands out of that hay or straw or whatever it is and come with me onto the playground to feast your eyes. You will not be sorry."

"It's not hay, Hoove. It's bulrush stalks. If you knew anything about the basket making habits of the Chumash tribe, you'd know that."

"Well, pardon me for not being a big fan of the weaving arts," the Hoove said. "I'm afraid I am just going to have to insist that you accompany me immediately."

Using all of his ghostly strength, he hooked his invisible arm through Billy's, flipped himself into hyperspeed and yanked Billy across the art room into the hall. A couple of the girls sniggered. To them, it looked like Billy was just stumbling across the room and out of the door. Little did they know he was being pulled by an actual ghost.

The Hoove pulled Billy down the hall and

out on to the playground. The bright sun made Billy squint as he looked around trying to find what the Hoove was talking about. All he saw were four kids from his class, supervised by Mr Wallwetter, practising for the bow and arrow demonstration. A target was pinned up to the back wall of the handball court, and one person was practising shooting a suction-cup-tipped arrow while the others looked on. Of course, that person was Rod Brownstone. Brownstone took aim and let go of the arrow just as Billy arrived. It wobbled through the air and landed on the ground, about a metre short of the target. Rod turned to Kayla Weeks, a shy, frizzy-haired redhead standing behind him.

"That was all your fault," he barked at her. "You bumped my arm."

"See, isn't that amazing," the Hoove said to Billy.

"I don't see anything amazing," Billy answered. "Just Brownstone being a bully, as usual."

The Hoove turned to Billy and looked closely into his face.

"You don't see her, do you?"

"Kayla? Sure I see her. It's hard to miss that whole mess of red hair."

"No, I mean *her*. Standing next to Kayla. With the beautiful brown eyes and shining, long black hair."

"You must be seeing things, Hoove. There's no one there but Mr Wallwetter and four kids from my class. And no one has long black hair. Unless you count the hair on Mr Wallwetter's arms, which I'd rather not."

"Concentrate, Billy," the Hoove said. "Feel her presence. Listen for the sound of her voice. And let me know when you see her."

Billy closed his eyes and concentrated. He didn't expect to see anything — he was just doing as he was told to get the Hoove off his back. But then, after a few seconds, he thought he heard something. It was a faraway rattle, like pebbles rolling in the sea, following by a faint drum beat and the sound of a girl's voice, chanting a strange melody. He opened his eyes, and saw her – a Native American girl, about his size, with long black hair and skin so transparent that she seemed to glow.

The minute she saw Billy gazing at her, an expression of fear darted across her face. As quickly as she had appeared, she disappeared into thin air, leaving nothing in her place but Brownstone's yapping voice.

Who was she? Where had she come from? And where had she gone?

Chapter 3

Billy stood on the playground, gazing into the empty space where the girl had been. The Hoove circled around him – actually whirled around him – talking non-stop.

"Did you see her?" he said. "Tell me you saw her. She was about my age, right? And her straight hair glistened in the sun. Did it or did it not? Come with me. You've got to help me find her."

"Hoove, the only place I'm going is back to the classroom that I left without permission."

"I can't believe you. You're honestly going to go weave some acorn basket instead of helping me, your pal, your roommate for the last few months? Think of everything I do for you."

"Like embarrassing me as I tripped over myself when you dragged me out of class?" Billy yelled. "Is that what you're talking about?"

Billy felt a hand on his shoulder and whipped around to see Mr Wallwetter looking him square in the eye.

"No, what I'm talking about is you leaving class without permission," he said, unaware that Billy was talking to his own personal ghost.

"Oh, Mr Wallwetter, sir. I'm so glad you're here."

"That's my job, Billy. To keep track of you wandering students. By my calculations, you're supposed to be in the art room."

"Your calculations are absolutely correct, sir. You are one fine calculator, if I do say so myself. If you were a machine, I could use you when I do my homework."

"You're sounding nervous, Billy Boy," the Hoove whispered. "You better come up with an explanation of why you're here. And whatever you do, do not mention the beautiful Native American princess."

"Of course I won't," Billy whispered back.

"Of course you won't what?" Mr Wallwetter asked.

"Um ... of course I won't leave class again without permission. I just needed some fresh air. All the fumes of the reeds and the straw were making my nose itch."

Mr Wallwetter eyed Billy suspiciously.

"What fumes?" he asked, looking sternly at Billy. "I didn't notice any fumes."

"I have this weird thing with my nose," Billy answered, making up a story on the spot. "It smells things that other noses don't. I'm proud of it and yet it's also a problem at the same time. But boy, is it powerful!"

A few of the kids from the playground had gathered around to see what the conversation was about. One of them was Rod Brownstone, who took the opportunity to butt in with his own observations.

"Mr Wallwetter," he said, using his official law enforcement tone of voice. "I have observed the suspect in question on the premises of his own house and I can report many things about him way stranger than his nose. For instance, just last night I observed his baseball bat moving around the room on its own."

Mr Wallwetter shifted his stern glance from Billy to Rod.

"That is an absurd story," he said without even a hint of a smile. "I suggest you calm down and mind your own business."

"I couldn't agree more," the Hoove sniggered, flicking Brownstone's earlobe in a really annoying manner.

"Cut it out, Broccoli," Rod snapped. "Stop messing with my ear."

"I am standing right here, Rod," Mr Wallwetter said. "And I see that Billy has both hands in his pockets. He didn't touch you."

"See? That's the kind of strangeness I'm

talking about," Rod answered, "which is why I have him under a twenty-four-hour watch."

The Hoove burst out laughing.

"I love it," he said. "We're making this guy seem like a total nut job."

Billy had trouble stifling his laugh. No matter how irritating the Hoove could be, he always stood up for Billy in the most creative ways.

"What I suggest, gentlemen, is that we end this conversation and you both go back to your assigned activities," Mr Wallwetter announced. "Rod, go help Kayla with her bow and arrow practice. And Billy, follow your itchy nose back to the art room."

Billy turned to go, but was stopped by the Hoove grabbing his shoulder.

"So you mean you're not going to help me find her?"

Mr Wallwetter noticed Billy pausing and raised an eyebrow. It was the kind of eyebrow raise that said, "If you don't do as I say, I will send you to the head teacher's office now." Billy hated to get in trouble, especially since his mother was the head teacher, so he plastered a huge smile on his face.

"Boy oh boy," he said. "I can't wait to get back to my basket weaving. I'm on my way RIGHT NOW."

Throwing the Hoove a determined glance, he turned on his heel and headed across the playground to the art room. Rod returned to bow and arrow practice under the careful watch of Mr Wallwetter. That left the Hoove all alone in the middle of the playground.

"Fine," he said to himself. "I'll find her by myself. I'm the one she'd want to feast her eyes on, anyway."

He floated across the yard, his dark eyes searching for any sign of her. As he passed the lunch area, he thought he saw a face peeking out from behind the water fountain. He zoomed over there, only to find a sweaty seventh grader sticking his whole face in the stream of water.

"You are disgusting, pal," he said. "That's why they invented the shower."

He thought he heard a little giggle coming from underneath the fountain. The Hoove swooped down to investigate and got there just in time to see two moccasins flying off into the air. He followed the moccasins across the yard to a group of students who were standing in front of a long roll of paper attached with clothespins to the chain-link fence. They were working on a mural that was going to be the backdrop for their Native American Night at the museum. One boy was painting a canoe, one of the girls was painting Chumash money, which was made out of sea shells, and Billy's friend Ricardo was painting the ocean and the California coastline where the Chumash lived.

The Hoove looked around for the Native American girl, but she was nowhere to be seen. It was as if she had vanished into thin air. He hovered above the mural, watching Ricardo add blue paint to the ocean waves. After a minute,

Ricardo put down his paintbrush, wiped his hands on his apron, and announced he was going to let the paint dry while he took a bathroom break. As the Hoove watched him jog across the yard, he saw something out of the corner of his eye. Something was moving in the mural itself!

The Hoove squinted his eyes and looked closely at the paper. It seemed as if the waves Ricardo had just painted were coming alive, rolling up to the sandy shore in the mural. With a sudden poof of pink light, the girl with the moccasins emerged from the paper, coming through the painted wave and taking her full shape in front of the mural. Unseen by the other children, she picked up Ricardo's brush and, with one or two flowing strokes, painted a dolphin jumping out of the water. It was the perfect touch to finish the mural.

"You are an amazement," the Hoove said to her.

She turned and gave him a startled look, then

dropped the brush and took off flying across the yard.

"Hey, don't disappear again!" he called after her. "I'm not going to bite you."

The Hoove threw himself into hyperglide and chased after her. She circled the entire playground with the Hoove following close behind. Finally, she zoomed through the chain-link fence and the Hoove pulled up short.

"Hey," he shouted. "Come back. I can't leave the yard. I mean, I would, but I can't."

She stopped in mid-air and spun around to look at him. Suddenly, the Hoove felt foolish. He didn't want to tell her that the Higher-Ups had grounded him and he could go no further than the school playground. When she saw that the Hoove wasn't following her, she cautiously floated back towards the chain-link fence and looked at him without speaking.

"Hoover Porterhouse the Third here," he said with a smile. "But you can call me the

Hoove. Or Mr Wonderful, whatever mood strikes your fancy."

She just kept staring at him without speaking, tilting her head this way and that, taking in every detail.

"OK, so you're the quiet type," he went on. "I'll do the talking for both of us. I know what you're thinking. It's very nice to meet me. Thank you. Most people feel that way."

Still not a word came out of her mouth, so the Hoove continued.

"You're probably wondering what a fun-loving ghost such as myself is doing spending the day at school when I don't have to be here. Well, let me just say, I possess the answer to this and all your other questions. I came here to work with my human pal Billy, who sadly lacks my ability to trip the light fantastic."

Her eyes grew wide as she listened to his words.

"Oh, I see you don't comprehend that. Allow me to continue. Billy can't seem to get the knack of the Chumash dance, which is not surprising, because it doesn't seem like a dance to me. More like hopping up and down like your feet are on fire."

A sudden frown crossed her face and she put her otherworldly hands on her hips.

"Those steps that you are making fun of are used by my people to awaken our spirit and teach respect for nature," she said.

"Hey, who doesn't respect nature? When I'm doing these steps, I am filled with mountains and rainbows and fields of green and all that stuff."

The Hoove let out an enthusiastic whoop and burst into his version of the Chumash dance he had practised with Billy the night before. He got a little carried away, and threw in some turkey trot steps as well. The result was a wild-looking waddle that bore only a vague resemblance to the original Chumash rain dance.

"Your fields would be much greener if you did it this way," she said.

Then she turned in a circle and with the grace of the wind, began moving her feet to the rhythm of drums she heard in her head. The Hoove stopped his crazy dance and stared at her, captured by the lightness of her steps. What had looked like just hopping to him suddenly appeared to be the most beautiful dance he had ever seen. He watched in silence. His usual river of words ran dry.

When she finished her dance, the girl just looked at him and smiled.

"That's pretty good," he said. "Where did you learn how to do that?"

"I am Princess Anacapa," she answered. "I am Chumash. I lived here in this valley with my tribe over two hundred years ago."

"Oh, an older woman. I'm just a kid; I'm only ninety-nine years old."

"Then you should respect your elders," she warned, wagging her finger at him.

"So am I safe to assume that you are a fellow ghost? Or in your case, ghost-ess?"

53

She giggled at the Hoove's little joke.

"Yes, I am a spirit, sent here to protect the land and sea and traditions of my people."

"So what, you just fly around from school to school helping kids learn native dances and weave baskets and stuff?"

"I live at the Natural History Museum," she said. "In the Chumash diorama. I spend much of my time standing next to the hairy buffalo, showing children who pass by what a Chumash village looks like. But I leave there when I am called into action."

"Oh, so that's why you're here."

"I received word from my Higher-Ups that the children of this school needed some help learning the Chumash ways."

"Oh man oh man, those Higher-Ups. Don't they drive you crazy?"

"No, I find them very kind and helpful."

"That is exactly what I was about to say. You took the words right off my tongue. Those Higher-Ups, they are one helpful bunch. If I had two words for them, it would be HELP and FULL."

"If you would be interested to learn more about the Chumash," Anacapa said, "I can teach you about our ways."

"Now that's a coincidence," the Hoove said. "Because believe it or not, I was just on my way to the library to check out every research book on the shelf about the Chumash. A person can't get enough of Native American history."

Anacapa seemed pleased with the Hoove's interest in her traditions.

"If you'd like to learn more about my people, you could come visit our diorama at the museum," she offered.

The Hoove was thrilled with her invitation. It was the first time in ninety-nine years that he had met a ghost of his own age, and it felt really good to be invited somewhere by her. He answered before he had time to think.

"I will be there," he said to her. "Give me the

time and date, and I'll materialize in all my glory."

"I have more work to do at the school today," Anacapa answered. "There is a boy here who is having great difficulty with the dance steps."

"Don't tell me. His first name starts with a B. Go easy on him. He's a great kid who tries so hard, but each of his feet has a mind of its own. They always go in two different directions."

"I will guide his feet on the day of the performance without him ever knowing I am there."

"Lucky him. Way to go, Billy Broccoli."

"I will go to this Billy Broccoli now, in his time of need. And I will see you tomorrow at our arranged hour."

"Great," the Hoove said. "I'll be there."

Anacapa drifted off across the playground. She was almost inside the building when the Hoove yelled out, "Wait a minute! When is our arranged hour, exactly?"

"Four o'clock," she called out.

"Of course it is! I'll be there or be square."

Anacapa floated through the doors and out of sight. The Hoove smiled to himself, feeling very excited about his plans for the next day.

But his excitement only lasted for one second. The next second it hit him that he was grounded, and the museum was off-limits. And not just a little off-limits, but by miles. This was going to require a conversation with the dreaded Higher-Ups. They were the only ones who could grant him the freedom to move beyond his travel zone.

"Hey, guys!" the Hoove called out to the clouds above. "A situation has arisen and I'm going to need to change my boundaries. I'd appreciate your cooperation. You can just say yes and I'll be on my way."

In response, a jagged bolt of lightning flashed across the sky, which was never a good sign.

Chapter 4

The Hoove was not the kind of ghost to take NO lightly. Even though the first sign from the Higher-Ups could only be interpreted as a big, fat NO, he was determined to convince them to let him visit Anacapa. But how?

He always got his best ideas in this thinking tree in the back garden. There was something about lying on the swaying top branch and gazing up at the sky that allowed his mind to be its most creative.

Quickly, he floated back inside the building and located Billy in the art room. Poor Billy was still trying to tame the reeds into a round bottom for his basket, but he wasn't having much luck.

To the Hoove, Billy's basket looked like a walrus with only one tusk.

"Hey Billy Boy, I don't know much about baskets, but I'm pretty sure they're supposed to have sides. The only thing you could do with that thing is float it in your bathtub."

"The Chumash didn't have bathtubs, Hoove. They used the river to bathe."

"I wonder if anyone asked the fish what they thought of that."

"I'm trying to concentrate on this, Hoove. I need to get this done by the lunch bell. And you're very distracting."

"That's what I do. I'm good at it."

"Can you disappear, please?"

"That's what I came to tell you. I'm leaving because I have to come up with a creative solution to a problem. Not that I'm asking you for help, but if you happen to have an idea or two about how I can convince the Higher-Ups to let me travel out of my zone to the museum tomorrow, I would consider listening."

"The museum? When did you ever want to go to the museum before?"

"Hey, I'm trying to expand myself. You can't knock a guy for that."

"Well, just tell the Higher-Ups that going to the museum is educational. And that it's important for your personal growth. Oh, and this will really get them. Tell them it's your responsibility to improve your mind."

"I'll use the trip home to see if your ideas fit into what I had in mind," the Hoove said. "And by the way, you just poked yourself with a reed and your finger's bleeding. You might want to get yourself a plaster. Oh, and remember Hoove's Rule Number 237. Never use a dinosaur plaster over the age of four."

"You actually have a rule for that?"

"There's a whole chapter in the Rule Book on plasters — the first of which is: do not use fluorescent pink on any body part that is exposed to the human eye."

Billy felt a hand, a human hand, on his shoulder.

"Are you all right?" Mrs Penny said, gazing down at his mess of a basket. "I notice that you were in full conversation with yourself."

"Oh, I'm just fine," Billy gulped. "I was just repeating the instructions for making this basket over and over to myself, so I wouldn't make a mistake."

Mrs Penny raised an eyebrow and glanced down at Billy's walrus-tusked basket.

"Well," she said cheerfully, "perhaps it's time to try some different instructions. Your basket seems to come from a whole different tribe."

The Hoove left Billy in the kindly hands of Mrs Penny and zoomed out of the art room. He glided down the hall, past Mr Wallwetter's room, and out of the front door of the school. As he flew, he glanced around, hoping to catch a glimpse of Anacapa, but no such luck.

He cruised over the rooftops of their neighbourhood, passing Mrs Pearson's house on the corner. As usual, she was riding around on her electric lawn mower like it was a wild ride at Disneyland. When he arrived in the Broccoli-Fielding back garden, he floated over to the twenty-metre-tall live oak tree that had been planted by his father on the day of his birth. It was his favourite place in the world to sit and think a problem through.

Settling on to the top branch, the Hoove put his mind to work. He knew that it was going to be difficult to convince the Higher-Ups to unground him for the day, so he was going to have to put his best case forward. He thought about how often they brought up his lack of responsibility and how they were hoping to see him grow more responsible each and every day. He decided he would lead off with that, explaining how a trip to the museum was responsible in every possible way.

"Hey, you guys," the Hoove called out to the sky. "Got a minute?"

At first nothing happened. Then he heard a

high-pitched whistle coming from the ground below. He squinted down to see where the whistle was coming from, but the only thing he saw was a slimy brown worm wiggling its way out of the ground. Soon a second worm wiggled its way into daylight, joining the original worm in whistling a tuneless melody.

The first one spoke, which was not easy because it was so tiny. But its voice reached him loud and clear.

"Hey, big boy," it said in a shrill voice. "Get down here."

"You talking to me?" the Hoove asked.

"We don't see anyone else in that tree," the second worm said. He was a sarcastic little worm.

"Wait ... are you ... I mean ... you're not ... I mean ... you couldn't be the Higher-Ups, could you?"

"No, we're worms. But we've been sent by them to deliver a message to you."

The Hoove floated off his branch and

cautiously descended, hovering just above the grass. He looked carefully at the two worms, trying to see exactly where their voices were coming from, but they looked just like any other slimy brown night crawlers.

"How do I know you're really their messengers?" he asked, casting them a suspicious look.

Suddenly, a huge glob of green slime shot out of the top of the first worm's head, sailed into the air, and formed the words, *"LISTEN UP! IT'S US!"*

The words dropped from the sky all over Hoove's head. It made him look like a gooey ghost from Mars.

"Is that proof enough for you?" the second worm asked.

"You're close to convincing me."

Suddenly, the second worm exploded, growing to the size of a large dog. It barked at the Hoove though its slimy mouth, and within seconds, returned to its original wormy self.

"OK, I'm convinced," the Hoove said. "I'm all ears. What do you have to tell me?"

"Excuse me," the first worm said. "You called us."

The Hoove took a deep breath and started talking faster than he ever had before.

"OK, this is my request," he began. "I'm having this enormous urge to improve my life and be responsible. I need to go to the museum, which is filled with educational opportunities for me to learn responsibility from the ground up. Especially the diorama section, where I can study the Chumash people. Let me tell you, they practically invented responsibility. They were not only responsible for the land, they were also champion basket-weavers, too. If they gave out trophies for basket weaving, those guys would have had a case full."

The second worm listened, then dived down into the earth. A few seconds later, he shot back up, straight as a stick.

"I have heard from the Higher-Ups. They

have the following message and I quote. 'GOOD TRY. WE KNOW ABOUT PRINCESS ANACAPA.'"

"Oh, that is so unfair," the Hoove said, putting his ghostly hands indignantly on his hips ... actually, through his hips. "You tell them that my desire to be more responsible has nothing to do with her."

"Here it comes again," the first worm said, and with that, his head exploded and another glob of green slime shot out. It floated in the air, this time forming the words, *"HORSE PUCKY!"*

The Hoove flew out of the way of the dripping slime before it had a chance to reach his face.

"You guys are insulting me," he complained loudly, looking up into the heavens. "All I'm asking for is a measly little day pass to go beyond my boundary to the museum. It's not like I'm asking to go to Ohio or Madagascar or anything. I mean, what does a guy have to do to get you to say yes?"

Now both worms started to whistle their shrill tuneless melody. As their voices grew higher and louder, they formed the words, "PROVE YOURSELF! PROVE YOURSELF! PROVE YOURSELF!"

They continued chanting those two words until the Hoove finally covered his ears and shouted, "All right. All right. I got the point. You can wiggle back into your wormhole now."

In an instant, the sound disappeared and the worms did, too, sinking into the ground as if they had never even been there.

The Hoove just stood there under his tree, shaking his head. The Higher-Ups could be so frustrating. They always told him what he had to do, but never explained how. Prove himself . . . what exactly did that involve? He didn't know how to prove himself. All he knew was that if he was ever to see Princess Anacapa again, he had to find a way.

Chapter 5

As Billy walked home from school that afternoon, the Hoove rushed up to him at the corner of his street, as out of breath as a ghost could be.

"What took you so long?" the Hoove panted. "I've been pacing back and forth here for an hour."

"I had to stay after school and redo the bottom of my basket. Turns out my reeds weren't flexible enough because they were too dry. So I had to soak them, and that took. . ."

"Will you stop with the basket–speak already?" the Hoove interrupted impatiently. "I have a big problemo in the Higher-Ups department and I need your help on it."

"Oh no," Billy said as they headed down Fairview to their house. "Did you insult them? I've told you a million times that you always have to treat them with respect."

"Would you please give your mouth a rest and start using your ears?"

"Fine. I'm listening. Oh wait, I can't find my key."

Billy fished around in his pocket for his house key until he remembered that his stepfather, Bennett, had tied it on to the inside zip of his rucksack with minted dental floss. "Dental floss is a multifunctional tool," he had said that morning. "It can stimulate your gums, clean between your teeth and make sure you never lose your key."

"Stop fidgeting with your rucksack," the Hoove said in an irritated voice. "I'm trying to tell you something of the utmost importance."

"To you, maybe. To me, it's more important to open the front door and see if my mum left out any peanut butter cookies for me."

The Hoove whooshed past Billy, flew through the door ... without opening it ... swooped into the kitchen, and returned with the plate of cookies — all in a split second. He opened the door for Billy and shoved the cookies into his hand.

"Here," he said. "Munch to your heart's content, as long as you can do two things at once, the second being LISTENING."

Billy flopped down on the living room couch and shoved two cookies into his mouth at once. There was nothing he loved better than his mum's buttery, nutty cookies. He would have preferred that they be accompanied by a glass of milk, but the Hoove had him cornered in the living room and was demanding his attention.

"Pro-theed," he said, shooting out a few crumbs that landed on his knee. He promptly scooped those up and popped them back in his mouth.

"So there's this girl," the Hoove began.

"Oh, you mean the disappearing one, who flies away when you even try and look at her."

"Maybe she flew away from you, Billy Boy, but she did not fly from me. Well, maybe at first, but not after she got to know me. In fact, she has invited me to her abode. The museum, to be exact."

"She lives in the museum? How does she eat?"

"She's a ghost, Billy Boy. We don't eat. We just make the quality of your life better. Now can we get back on track here?"

"It's your conversation, Hoove. I'm just sitting here enjoying my cookies, listening up a storm."

"So as I was saying, she lives in the museum, in the Chumash diorama next to the hairy buffalo."

"So what was she doing at my school?"

"That's your first good question, Billy Boy. Those peanut butter nuggets must be firing up your brain. As it turns out, it is her responsibility to see that the traditions of the Chumash people

71

are respected and carried on. And she protects the land and the sea around these parts. She's like a one-woman Environmental Protection Agency. And by the way, did I mention she has beautiful black hair."

"Aha," Billy said. "Now we get to the real reason you're so interested in her."

"What are you saying? I'm not a tree hugger? I've hugged more pine than you can shake an oak branch at."

"Good for you. So what's your point?"

"The point is that I told Anacapa ... that's her name ... that I'd meet her at the museum tomorrow at four o'clock. She's going to give me the super deluxe tour of the diorama, teach me about the Chumash ways. And listen to this, Mr Broccoli — she has also agreed to be your personal dance instructor. Come Friday night at your performance, she is going to guide your feet to perfection."

"Cool. My feet could use some perfection. This all sounds great. So what's the problem?"

"Use your head, buddy. The museum is off-limits for me. I requested a special pass from the Higher-Ups. And can you believe it, they did not say yes. They have the nerve to ask me to prove myself yet again."

"You better get going on that," Billy said. "Tick tock. You don't have much time."

"I'm going to start right away. I only have one more question. What do you think I should do to prove myself?"

"Well, what's the most responsible thing you can think of that would really get their attention?"

The Hoove looked blankly around the living room, searching for ideas. Responsibility did not come easily to him.

"Well," he stammered. "I could volunteer to vacuum the rug. Nah, I don't do well with dust."

He looked out of the front window.

"I could mow the lawn. Nah, grass gives me a rash."

Billy could see that the Hoove was running out of ideas before he even started. They looked around the room desperately. Out of the corner of his eye, he saw their grey cat, Stormy, who had just recently had a litter of kittens, slink into the living room. She came slinking up to the Hoove's leg and rubbed against it. Even though Stormy couldn't feel his leg, the cat sensed Hoove's presence. They were good friends.

"Hey, wait a minute. An idea has just occupied my brain," the Hoove said. "I'm going to give Stormy a bath. I bet that would score me some major points. Taking care of our animal brothers and sisters has got to rank high on the responsibility scale."

Before Billy could point out that cats aren't really big on taking baths, the Hoove had reached down and scooped Stormy up in one arm and stroked her head with his free hand. Stormy purred happily.

"Let's go get you all spiffed up," he said, heading for the bathroom. "Maybe you'd even enjoy a bubble bath, each delicate bubble caressing your fur."

Billy followed the Hoove into the bathroom, watching as he turned on the water in the bathtub. The room filled with steam and created a mist on the mirror. Soon the mist thickened into a fog so thick it completely covered the mirror. Then a single finger appeared in front of the mirror, writing words on its steamy surface.

"*Cats give themselves baths,*" the finger wrote. "*That's why they have bumpy tongues.*"

Billy stared at the words in amazement. As many times as he had seen a message come from the Higher-Ups, it always filled him with awe to see a new one arrive. The Hoove was less impressed.

"You folks up there are stepping all over my creativity," he yelled into to the misty air. "How many ideas can a guy have?"

The mirror fogged up again, and the lone finger wrote out one single word.

"*MORE*" was all it said.

Chapter 6

The Hoove floated back and forth across the bathroom, sighing dramatically. The Higher-Ups were really making him work to get the pass to go see Anacapa. He knew he was going to have to come up with a better idea than bathing cats.

"OK," he said to Billy. "You're the smarty-pants here. What's big and impressive? Quick. Name three things."

"Mount Everest, the Statue of Liberty and a black stretch limousine with purple neon lights inside," Billy suggested.

"Not helpful," the Hoove answered. "I can't climb Mount Everest, because my mountain climbing shoes are in permanent storage. And I can't even leave this neighbourhood, so that pretty much makes the Statue of Liberty a big no-go. Which leaves the limousine. You don't happen to have a black stretch limousine parked in your drive, do you?"

"Nope, but Bennett walked to work today, so his ice-blue people carrier with the '*Stamp Out Cavities*' bumper stickers is there."

The Hoove stopped pacing and looked up. "OK, maybe I can work with that," he said.

"Actually, those bumper stickers are pretty cool. They're shaped like toothbrushes and they glow in the dark."

"Not the bumper stickers, Billy Boy. I'm talking about the car. You know how Bennett likes to keep it all shiny and neat. How about if yours truly turns that vehicle into a monument of clean?"

He looked skyward and grinned.

"A one-man car wash," he shouted. "If that doesn't get me to the museum, then I don't know what will!"

The Hoove was so excited by his own idea that

before Billy could even answer, he was through the bathroom door, sailing across the house and out into the driveway. He circled Bennett's car three times, checking out its condition, and had the whole situation assessed by the time Billy got there.

"We got ourselves a layer a dust that looks like this car just got back from the desert," he said. "The rims could use a good scrubbing, which I am highly capable of doing. And surprise of surprises, the floor on the passenger side is knee deep in candy wrappers. It seems our dear Dr Dentist doesn't always practise what he preaches. The guy sneaks Baby Ruths like they're going out of style."

Billy laughed. Somehow, he couldn't imagine Bennett Fielding stuffing his face with decay-causing sugary treats. No wonder the man carried a lifetime supply of dental floss on his belt.

The Hoove rolled up his sleeves and started barking out commands.

"Billy, I'm going to need you to run in the house and bring me the following: one bucket of soapy warm water, a large sponge, a vacuum and a gigantic plastic bag. We've already got the hose in the front garden."

"Aye, aye, captain," Billy said, throwing out a mock salute.

Billy took off into the house and returned shortly, carrying all the necessary items.

"I found everything but a sponge," he said. "There was one in the sink, but it still had little bits of last night's dinner in it. I don't think leaving Bennett's car smelling like meatballs in tomato sauce is going to help your cause."

"Hey, don't worry yourself, Broccoli. I will happily become the sponge. Watch and be amazed."

The Hoove bent himself in half and started to spin in the air. He spun so fast that he shape-shifted, his arms and legs folding in tight against his body. After a minute, all you could see of him was a basketball-size circle. Spinning faster and faster, he shrank into the size of a softball and immediately did a cannonball into the soapy bucket of water.

"Ow!" his voice echoed from inside the bucket.

"What happened? Did you hit the bottom of the pail?" Billy called out.

"No, the soap got in my eyes," a bubbly voice answered. "I forgot about that sting. I haven't had to wash my face in the last ninety-nine years."

The sponge-shaped Hoove catapulted out of the bucket and plopped itself on to the hood of Bennett's car, rolling vigorously from side to side.

"Hey, this isn't so bad," the Hoove shouted. "It's like surfing in the ocean, except without a wave."

"Don't celebrate yet," Billy said. "You missed a spot on the windscreen. I think it's a bird dropping."

The sponge stopped dead in its tracks and the Hoove's head popped out of the ball shape.

"I don't do poop," he said.

"Fine. I guess you don't really want to see Anacapa, then. Do you really think the Higher-Ups are going to overlook an obvious mound of doo-doo?"

"You're the mound of poop," a voice said from behind Billy. "And by the way, who are you talking to?"

It was Rod Brownstone, who had emerged from his house carrying his ever-present walkie-talkie.

"I've been watching you," he said to Billy, "and it looks to me like you're talking to this piece of junk car. Normal people don't have conversations with vehicles. I'm going to have to report this to the officials."

"I can talk to anything I want, Brownstone," Billy said. "As long as it's not you. And if I ever do talk to you, then I should get a ticket for disturbing the peace."

From inside the sponge, the Hoove let out a huge guffaw.

"Good one, Billy Boy. You show that piece of baloney who's boss."

The Hoove was laughing so hard that he skidded across the hood of the car, emitting soap suds as he sailed along the metal. Watching the sponge seemingly move on its own, Brownstone's eyes grew wide with disbelief. Billy grabbed the Hoove-sponge and started to rub it over the windscreen, flashing Rod a sheepish smile as if everything were normal.

"Hey, you're tickling me," the Hoove laughed. "Cut it out."

But Billy couldn't cut it out. He had to make it look like he was controlling the sponge, not the other way around. The Hoove, never one to like being pushed around, resisted and hurled himself in the opposite direction. He tugged so hard that he pulled Billy to the back of the car. Billy just continued to grin at Rod and pretended to be very involved in scrubbing the rear door. With another fierce tug, the Hoove pulled Billy around to the other side panel. Billy had no choice but to follow, being careful that he didn't trip over his own feet.

"What's wrong with you?" Brownstone asked. "You look like your pants are on fire."

"When you have the urge to soap up a car, you just have to go with it," Billy answered. "I'm sure you know the feeling."

"You and your stupid soap suds are weird, Broccoli. In fact, I'm getting out of here right away before your weirdness rubs off on me."

As Rod turned to head back into his house, the Hoove couldn't resist. He left the car and flew over to Brownstone, hovering just above his head. Contracting his whole body, he squeezed out a blast of soapy water that sprayed all over Rod's hair. Rod whipped around and shot Billy a nasty look.

"That's a violation, Broccoli. Assault with a soapy sponge. You're going to pay for this."

He hunkered off into the house, probably to get his codebook and look up the penalty for assault with a soapy sponge. The Hoove roared with laughter.

"You're laughing now," Billy said, "but you won't be laughing when the Higher-Ups punish you for that little move."

"Come on, they must have a sense of humour. Besides, I'm doing a bang-up job here, they've got to respect that. Hand me that Dustbuster, Billy. I'm ready to take on the interior."

The Hoove popped back to his normal shape, and Billy handed him the Dustbuster. The Hoove took it and shot through the front door of the car. Unfortunately, the mini-vacuum stayed on the outside and fell to the ground. When Billy reached down to pick it up, he saw that what had been one mini-vacuum was now two half vacuums. Neither one of them worked.

"Hey, you broke this," he called to the Hoove. "How am I going to explain this to my mum?"

The Hoove wasn't listening. He was zipping around the inside of the car, gathering up the candy wrappers.

"I'm going to throw these out of the window," he called to Billy. "You hold the plastic bag and I'll toss them in."

He reached over to the electric window controls that were on the centre console. What he didn't realize was that the button he was pressing was not the window control. It was the parking brake release.

The car started to roll down the drive, slowly at first, then picking up speed as it went downhill.

"Hoove!" Billy shouted. "The car's moving! Put on the emergency brake!"

The Hoove looked desperately around. All the buttons on the console looked the same to him.

"I don't know where it is on a modern car," he called, panic in his voice.

Billy raced alongside the moving car, pulling on the door handle as he ran. He jumped inside the car and shouted for the Hoove to move over to the passenger side. Holding the steering wheel with two hands, he slammed his foot on the regular brake, which gave him a moment to engage the emergency brake. The car came to a screeching halt. They were in the middle of the street, but at least they hadn't hit anything.

"Is this what you call being responsible?" Billy said angrily. "You could have caused an accident and got me in big trouble."

"You know that 'trouble' part you're talking about?" the Hoove said. "Look over your left shoulder. I think it's coming your way."

Billy glanced over his shoulder and saw his mother pulling up in her car, with Breeze sitting in the seat next to her. They both had a horrified look on their faces. His mum practically flew out of her car.

"Billy Everett Broccoli!" she shouted. "What are you doing driving Bennett's car?"

Billy rolled down the window.

"This isn't what it looks like, Mum."

Breeze had got out of the car and joined her mother.

"You're eleven, pipsqueak. You can't drive. You have a hard time combing your hair, let alone operating a motor vehicle. You are so grounded."

"Mum, don't listen to her," Billy begged. "I can explain."

"There are no explanations for this, Billy. I have seen everything I need to see. Go to your room immediately."

"And be prepared to stay there for seven years," Breeze added.

"Breeze, I'll handle this, thank you," Ms Broccoli-Fielding said.

Billy slid from the seat and headed into the house. The Hoove was right behind him.

"This is tough turn of events," the Hoove said. "But we'll get out of this."

"You just got me in it," Billy said, marching down the hall to his room. "Why is it that whatever you do ends up to be a disaster for me?"

"I was just trying to be responsible," the Hoove said. "And hey, you have to admit, I did a pretty good job. That car looks beautiful, even if it is in the middle of the street."

"Oh really? Why don't you ask the Higher-Ups what they think?"

"As a matter of fact, I will do that immediately. And I am convinced that they will see that underneath this slight glitch, what I did was worthy of a trip to the museum."

The Hoove followed Billy into his room. Billy flicked on the light switch, but instead of the ceiling light going on, instead the ceiling lit up with a thousand twinkling stars.

"You see," the Hoove said to Billy. "They're glowing at me. Hoove's Rule Number 419: stars are always a positive sign."

"I think you'd better scratch that one right out of the Rule Book," Billy said. "Take another look."

The Hoove looked up at the ceiling again. The stars had moved their positions, forming a sparkling constellation of two simple words: "*REQUEST DENIED.*"

Chapter 7

The Hoove spent half of that evening pacing back and forth in Billy's room in the way that ghosts pace, which is to say, just above the carpet.

"Those Higher-Ups frustrate me so much," he kept muttering, as Billy sat at his desk trying to study for his geography test the next day.

"Yeah, well, you're doing the same to me, Hoove. I have to learn all the capital cities of Africa for a pop quiz tomorrow and your complaining is not helping my concentration."

"I say we go out for some fresh air," the Hoove suggested. "These four walls are driving me crazy, and I need to calm myself down."

"I'd like some fresh air," Billy answered, "but

because of a certain car incident caused by a certain flakey ghost I'm forced to know, I am grounded in this room until I grow a moustache. Which won't be until I'm at least eighteen, because I'm having a slow growth spurt."

"You know, Billy Boy, moustaches are overrated. And so is being tall."

"That's easy for you to say, Hoove. No one sees you."

"That is incorrect. Anacapa saw me, and apparently she liked what she saw. And now, I can't keep my appointment with her, and among other things, I will never find out exactly when the Chumash people began using corn for pancakes."

"That shows how much you know, Hoove. The Chumash used acorns ground up to make mush and soup, which they ate on a daily basis."

"My point exactly, Billy Boy. These are the scintillating facts I would know if I could get to the museum. Besides, what's Anacapa going to think of me if I don't show up?"

"She'll think that you're a no-show, which, by the way, you are most of the time. You've got to admit, Hoove, you're not exactly the essence of reliability."

"You are correct, sir. But that was the old Hoove. You are speaking to a brand-new me."

"Oh really. And what exactly is causing this total turnaround?"

The Hoove stopped floating around the room and looked squarely at Billy. A look of serious determination crossed his face. Billy had never seen him assume that expression before and couldn't imagine what the Hoove was going to say next.

"You have to understand what it's been like for me, for the last ninety-nine years," the Hoove began. "Every ghost friend I have is a thousand years older than me. It's like hanging around with your great-grandfather, times nine. They're not exactly the fun guys."

Billy put his pencil down and spun his chair around. There was something in the Hoove's tone of voice that sounded so sincere. There was none of his usual swagger.

"I'm your friend," Billy told him. "And we're close to the same age."

"It's not the same," the Hoove said. "First of all, we're in two different worlds. And second of all, you're the only one who can see me, which is very limiting in a social situation. With Anacapa, I have a chance to have a friend who's really like me."

"You mean dead?"

"That's one way to say it, and very uncalled for. Another way to say it is that we are both citizens of the spiritual plane. We're like two peas in a pod. Or two kernels of corn on a husk. Or two spears of asparagus in a bunch. Two carrots. . ."

"Enough with the vegetables, Hoove. I get the picture."

"So you can understand, then, why I don't want to miss this appointment. Anacapa does not seem like the kind of person who takes being stood up lightly."

The Hoove flopped down on Billy's bed and let out a long sigh, which filled the room with cold air. A scent of tart oranges wafted from him.

"I'm sorry, Hoove," Billy said softly. "I wish I could help you."

The Hoove just lay there with his eyes closed, still as a sardine in a can. Suddenly, his eyes opened wide as he shot up into the air.

"That's it," he shouted. "That's the answer. I can't believe I'm saying this, but *you* are the answer, Billy Boy. You're the key that will unlock this problem."

"I'm not liking the sound of this," Billy said, fear overtaking his sympathy.

"Trust me," the Hoove said. "This will be as simple as rolling out of bed and brushing your teeth. All you have to do is go to the museum tomorrow at four o'clock. Find Anacapa in her diorama. And tell her that I had an unexpected turn of events . . . um . . . that my leg fell off and I have to go find it . . . and I can't make it."

"You expect me to say that with a straight face?" Billy said. "I can't."

"What's the problem? Is it the leg thing? Maybe you're right. That is a little extreme. OK, tell her instead that my hand fell off. That's much more believable."

"I don't think she wants to hear about your missing body parts, Hoove."

"OK, tell her anything. But deliver this message. Ask her if she'll meet me at the movies."

"You want me to ask her out on a date for you?"

"No, it's not a date. It's a Get to Know You kind of thing. Tell her I'll be waiting for her Friday at noon. Outside Cinema Three. Make sure you don't say Cinema Nine, because that's off-limits for me. Great, now we have a plan."

"Except for one small thing, Hoove. I can't go to the museum for you, because I'm grounded. Remember?"

All the enthusiasm left the Hoove's body, and he seemed to deflate like a popped balloon.

"You were my last hope," he said, flopping back on the bed. "Now I'll never have a real friend."

The Hoove put his hand up to his forehead, wobbled unsteadily for a moment, then seemed to faint onto the rug.

"Hoove, are you OK?" Billy asked.

"As OK as a guy can be who is feeling great amounts of loneliness. But don't bother yourself with me. You go on with what's important to you, like that geography test of yours. I'll be fine. If you don't mind, I'll just lie here for a while and try to get over my disappointment."

Billy sighed. "Hoove, I already explained this to you. I'm grounded. I can't go anywhere. Not to baseball practice. Not to Ricardo's house. And not to the museum. I'm stuck here at home."

"You could try, Billy. You could tell your parents you have to go to the museum for educational purposes. Which is true. You're not telling a fib. I mean, you are studying the Chumash and all."

"My mum will say no. She wasn't kidding around when she saw me behind the steering wheel."

The Hoove got up off the bed and floated over to Billy, putting both his transparent hands on Billy's shoulders.

"Hoove's Rule Number 437," he said. "You don't know unless you try."

"OK, OK, I'll try."

"Attaboy. And while you're at it, don't forget Rule Number 612. Don't try too hard. Parents always know when you're desperate."

Billy got up and headed towards the door of his room. As he pulled it open and stepped into the hall, he heard the Hoove's final advice.

"And definitely follow Rule Number 43. Never come back without a win."

Billy felt like the Hoove's entire future happiness depended on him. As he approached the kitchen, it felt like he was carrying the weight of a truckload of asteroids on his back. He pushed open the door a crack and saw his parents deep in conversation, with Breeze sitting nearby at her laptop, looking uninterested. He paused and listened to the conversation.

"No, Bennett," his mother was saying. "I don't think Billy's punishment is too severe. You have to understand, I saw him behind the wheel of a car in the middle of the street."

Billy didn't move a muscle, hoping that the next thing he heard would be Bennett telling his mum that just this one time, they should let him off without a punishment. After all, it was the first time he had taken the car out on his own.

But sadly for Billy, he heard no such thing.

"I guess you're right, Charlotte," Bennett said. "The boy has to learn a lesson. The automobile is not a toy."

Billy knew he had his work cut out for him. He took a deep breath to prepare himself, threw back his shoulders and marched into the kitchen, assuming a confident air.

"Hello, folks," he said. "What's for dinner?"

"Bread and water for you," Breeze said.

"Go back to your homework, Breezy," her father said. "We're handling the situation just fine."

"I'm not doing homework," Breeze answered. "I'm working on the lyrics of my new song, 'Loving You is Like Scraping My Elbow'."

"Listening to you is like spraining my ankle," Billy shot back. He chuckled vigorously but stopped when he realized he was the only one chuckling.

Breeze rolled her eyes at him, which wasn't easy to do, because she was wearing so much mascara that her eyelids were very heavy.

"I've got to hand it to you, pipsqueak," she said. "It takes a lot of nerve for a guy in your position to come in here making a joke. Apparently, you don't realize how big the doghouse is that you're in."

"I can be here if I want," Billy said.

"Nuh-uh, pipsqueak. I hear that you're

banished to your room for the next thirty years."

"Breeze, I have an important matter to discuss with my mum and Bennett," Billy said. "And if you don't mind, I'd like to do it in private, please."

"Fine with me, Mr Stunt Driver. I have to call the other girls in the band, anyway. Maybe they can help me think of a word that rhymes with *elbow*. A songwriter's job is never done."

Breeze took her laptop and her attitude and left, leaving Billy standing awkwardly in front of his mother and Bennett.

"I assume you're here to apologize for the extremely poor judgement you used this afternoon," his mother began.

"That is exactly why I'm here, Mum."

"Good for you, son," Bennett said. "It takes a big man to acknowledge he was wrong."

"Not only do I acknowledge it, I am shocked at myself," Billy said, clasping his hands in a very apologetic gesture. He had considered trying to tell them what had really happened, but in the end, he rejected the idea. Bringing up the existence of his personal ghost would have him heading back to his room before he even got his request out.

"So now that we've got past the apology stage," Billy continued, "I have a request to make. I would never ask this in a million years if it weren't so important to my success in school. And I think we all know that excelling in school is number one on my To-Do List."

"Sounds to me like someone is buttering us up like a turkey on Thanksgiving," Mrs Broccoli-Fielding said. Being a school head teacher, she had a lot of experience with kids trying to sweet talk her, and she had a "butter-up detector" the size of Texas.

"Here's the thing," Billy said. "You know that Friday is our performance of our Native American Night celebration at the museum."

"If what you're about to ask is can you still participate in that," Bennett said, "the answer is yes. Your mother and I have agreed to let you attend. But after that, you are back to being grounded for the next two weeks."

"Then let me get right to the point," Billy said, assuming from Bennett's tone of voice that the answer to his request was going to be a firm no. "I need to go to the museum tomorrow at four. I know I'm grounded, but there's information there that I need. It will only take me seventeen minutes."

"What kind of information only takes seventeen minutes to absorb?" his mother asked. She was not easy to fool.

"I need to study the details of the Chumash diorama," he said. His parents were looking at him quizzically, so he kept talking, trying to make his case even stronger. "Specifically, I would like to examine the hairy buffalo and the princess standing next to him, to see how they coexisted."

"There's a hairy buffalo at the museum?" Bennett asked, his ears perking up with curiosity.

"I hear it's extremely hairy," Billy nodded, "which is why I need to see it for myself."

"And you can't see this buffalo in a book or online?" his mum asked.

"Mum, nothing can replace standing in front of him, the buffalo in three dimensions. I can picture it now – the buffalo, his hair blowing in the breeze, and the princess, her hair . . . um . . . blowing in the breeze, too."

"Scientifically speaking," Bennett said, "there is no breeze inside the diorama."

"Unless, of course, they have a fan in there," Billy retorted. "Which I will never know unless I go."

"Very good thinking, Bill," Bennett said with a nod of approval.

Billy's mum was looking at him with one eyebrow raised. It was the look she always gave him when she suspected he had done something wrong. Billy knew he had to make his big move now, or the answer was going to be no.

"Mum," he said. "I want history to come alive for me. I want to be one with the Chumash. I want to feel their spirit in me. You know, taste the acorns. Smell the buffalo."

"Feel the breeze," his mother added, still suspicious.

"Yes! Exactly! I'm so glad you understand, Mum."

She glanced over at Bennett. He was smiling.

"I remember having the same enthusiasm for learning when I was a young man," he said with a faraway look in his eyes. "The first time I ever held a dental drill in my hand, it was as if every dentist who ever lived was speaking to me. I could feel their spirit in me through the vibration of the drill."

Billy didn't say a word. If there was one thing he knew, it was when to keep quiet in front of your parents. He could feel a decision coming, almost taste the thrill of victory. If only his mother's eyebrow would go back down to its normal position.

"I'll drive him," Bennett said to Billy's mum. "And I'll set my stopwatch to exactly seventeen minutes. Honestly, Charlotte, I don't know how we can say no to such an enthusiasm for learning."

"He's right, Mum," Billy threw in. "You don't want to squelch my enthusiasm for learning. After all, you are an educator."

Billy watched as his mother's eyebrow slowly, slowly, slowly moved down on her face until it was back in its normal position. He knew what that meant.

"All right," she said. "I'm going to make an exception this one time. As long as you understand, Billy, that what you did was wrong and there have to be consequences for that."

"Consequences are my middle name," Billy said, giving them each a fast hug. "Thanks, guys."

He turned on his heel, bounded out of the kitchen and down the hall. His knew he had to beat it out of there fast, before his mother changed her mind. He reached his room and threw open the door. The Hoove was hanging upside down from the ceiling light fixture, swinging sadly back and forth.

"I did it!" Billy exclaimed. "We're on for tomorrow!"

The Hoove let go of the light fixture and rocketed into the carpet, bouncing up again to throw his transparent arms around Billy, spinning him in circles. As Billy twirled around, he noticed Breeze standing in the hallway, staring at him like he had lost his mind. How was he going to explain this to her?

"Velcro," he said to her.

"OK," she answered. "Now I know you're officially crazy."

"Velcro rhymes with elbow," he said. "Loving you is like scraping my elbow, but trust me baby, I'm sticking to you like Velcro."

Breeze's eyes grew wide, and she forgot all about Billy's little happy dance with the air.

"That's actually brilliant," she said, dashing

to her room to grab her ever-present phone. "Wait until I tell the girls."

She disappeared into her room, and Billy turned to the Hoove.

"You heard the lady," he said. "I'm brilliant."

"Let's just hope you can be half that brilliant with Anacapa tomorrow," the Hoove said. "I have a lot riding on you."

Billy was bursting with confidence. On the heels of sweet-talking both his parents and Breeze, he was feeling like a man with a golden tongue. Nothing could go wrong. He would explain everything to Anacapa with charm and ease.

Which only goes to show how much he knew.

Chapter 8

The next morning, Billy awoke to a buzz of activity. The Hoove was in the wardrobe, spinning around like a pinwheel in the wind, and muttering to himself.

"What are you doing in there, Hoove?" Billy yawned as he rubbed the sleep from his eyes. "It sounds like the wardrobe door is going to come right off its hinges."

"While you were counting sheep, I've been in here developing my plan for how I'm going to wrangle that pass from the Higher-Ups," the Hoove answered. "I can hold Anacapa off for a day, but sooner or later, I am going to need to visit that museum. Sooner is what I'm sure we'd both prefer. At least I know I would."

The Hoove zoomed out of the wardrobe through the keyhole and over to Billy. "Consequently, I have made a list that includes every responsible activity a ghost, namely me, could participate in. Check this out, Billy Boy. It's a little bit of perfection, if I say so myself."

The Hoove handed Billy a long piece of toilet roll filled with his scratchy handwriting.

"It looks like a chicken stepped in some ink and walked across this," Billy said. "Is this supposed to be handwriting?"

"You're not worthy to hold my list." The Hoove grabbed the toilet paper back from Billy, almost tearing it in half. "I will read it to you myself."

"Be careful, you're about to lose one of the squares."

"Instead of employing your bad sense of humour, employ your ears," the Hoove snapped. Then he began to read. "One. I will locate all elderly ladies within my boundary and help them carry their grocery bags filled with prune juice and cat food. Two. I will return every lost dog to its rightful owner, even if it has fleas. Three. I will make banana cupcakes for Amber Brownstone's bake sale. With yellow sprinkles on top."

"How do you know she's having a bake sale?" Billy asked.

"We ghosts know everything. We are all-seeing and all-knowing."

"If you know so much, how come you don't know how to convince the Higher-Ups to spring you just this once?"

"Hence the list, Mr Broccoli. When I get finished with my perfect day, no one in this world or the other one will be able to say no to Hoover Porterhouse the Third. I will have proved myself responsible beyond a shadow of doubt. When you see Anacapa, tell her to meet me tomorrow at the mall. Outside Cinema Three. That's within my boundaries. And there I will surprise her with the big news."

"What news?"

"That I will be there Friday night at the

performance. I will tell her that I wouldn't miss the Native American celebration for all the candyfloss at a carnival."

"But Hoove, what if they don't offer you the pass by then? You're promising something you may not be able to deliver."

"You, my friend, are a negative thinker. I, on the other hand, am filled with positivity. So go, deliver the message. I've got a flock of seniors to escort."

The Hoove flew out of the window without so much as a goodbye. As Billy sauntered into the bathroom to brush his teeth, he kept thinking about how confident the Hoove was that he would get to the museum to see Anacapa. He had never before shown such determination to complete a plan.

On the walk to school, Billy caught a glimpse of the Hoove at the corner of Moorepark and Fairview. He was hovering next to an older woman who was waiting for the red light to change. She had a big German shepherd on a lead, and the dog was sniffing the air in a very agitated fashion. He obviously sensed the Hoove's presence, but the Hoove didn't seem to notice that the dog was trying to locate him. He just waved at Billy cheerfully.

"This kindly grandmother type is on her way to the grocery store," he called. "I'm going to see that she gets there and back safely."

Dogs have very good hearing, and he must have detected the sound of the Hoove's voice, because he started to bark like crazy. He tugged so hard on the lead that it almost pulled the woman off her feet. The Hoove reached out and caught her just before she fell.

"See!" he shouted to Billy. "My first good deed already accomplished."

Billy just shook his head and walked on. He had a big day at school and he couldn't be bothered with the Hoove's antics. He not only had to perfect his Chumash dance, but he also had to finish his basket and put together his costume. Ruby Baker had told him that

Chumash men wore very little, but he had told her in no uncertain terms that he was not about to appear shirtless in front of everyone at the museum. They decided that they'd both wear beige shirts and trousers, and Ruby was bringing in two eagle feathers that they could use for hair decoration.

The day flew by. Occasionally, Billy thought about the Hoove and wondered how his day of good deeds was going, but mostly, he kept his head down and concentrated on all he had to do. He was pleased when, by the last rehearsal of the day, his dancing had improved so much that he only stepped on Ruby's toes three times.

After school, Bennett was waiting in his people carrier in front of the school as Billy ran down the steps. He climbed into the front seat, snapped in his safety belt and turned to Bennett.

"Would you rather have me drive?" he said with a chuckle. "I now have experience."

Bennett threw back his head and laughed.

"One thing I can say about you, Bill, is that you have your mother's sense of humour."

"And the one thing I can say about you, Bennett, is that you get me," Billy said. "Thanks for that."

The museum was almost a half an hour's drive from Moorepark Middle School. They had to go on two different motorways, and the traffic was bumper to bumper. Billy kept eyeing the clock on the dashboard as it approached four o'clock.

"How much longer before we're there?" he asked nervously. The Hoove had explained that Anacapa was expecting him at exactly four o'clock.

"Never can tell with Los Angeles traffic," Bennett said. "But what's the rush? Since we're having such a bonding experience, why don't we play a game to pass the time? I've got a fun one. First person who sees a licence plate that starts with an X says 'X-ray'. Wait, make that 'dental X-ray'."

Bennett threw back his head and laughed again. Not a minute had gone by before he hollered, "Dental X-ray!"

"Where?" Billy asked. "I don't see an X licence plate."

"There wasn't one." Bennett flashed a oddly mischievous smile. "'Dental X-ray' is just fun to say. I love those words."

It was one minute after four when they pulled up in front of the Natural History Museum, an impressive stone building covered by a carved dome. Billy was as nervous as a cat as Bennett surveyed the car park for a good space.

"How about if you just drop me off in front," he suggested. "We can meet in the diorama hall."

"What's the rush?" Bennett asked.

"I want to use every one of my seventeen minutes to the fullest," Billy said. "I just can't wait to absorb all that Chumash-ness."

Bennett reached out and tousled Billy's hair.

"Gotta love your enthusiasm," he said. "I

should be there in five or ten minutes. Don't get lost. It's a big place inside."

"Don't worry about me," Billy said, climbing out of the car. "I'll find it. I have the sense of direction of a bald eagle hunting for salmon."

Billy raced up the front steps and into the main hall. A grey-haired, uniformed guard was standing just inside the door.

"I know what you're looking for," he said in a loud voice. "The Hall of Dinosaurs. That's what youngsters your age like. Yup, if there's one thing I know, it's you youngsters."

"Actually, sir, I need to find the dioramas," Billy said.

"What's that?" the guard asked, turning up his hearing aid. "You have diarrhea? Then you'll need to find the bathrooms down the hall and on your left."

"Diarrhea, diarrhea!" Billy heard a little voice say.

He turned around to see a kid of about five in floppy shorts and mismatched shoes standing at the information booth, holding his mother's hand.

"Shhh, Harry," his mother said. "That's not an appropriate word for a museum."

"But that big boy has diarrhea," Harry giggled. "That guard said it. And he knows the museum rules."

"Actually," Billy said, raising his voice so the guard could hear him. "What I am looking for is the hall with the dioramas of the Chumash tribe."

"Oh, why didn't you say that in the first place," the guard said. "Let me look up where it is. I'm a new volunteer here."

While the guard rummaged through his worn map of the museum, Billy tapped his foot nervously. He was on a seventeen-minute clock, and he could feel the minutes ticking down. He was so relieved when Harry's mother touched him on the shoulder.

"Why don't you just follow us," she said. "What you're looking for is the California

History Hall, which is down that hall past the Gem and Mineral Hall. I know where it is because those dioramas are Harry's favourite thing in the whole museum."

"Yeah," Harry said, pulling his finger out of his nose. "I like the hairy buffalo best. He's standing right in front of the teepee, which is almost as fun to say as diarrhea."

"Harry, honey, that's not a teepee," his mum explained. "The Chumash lived in round, thatched homes called *aps*."

"Hey, I'd love to hang out with you guys and discuss Chumash architecture," Billy said, "but I'm in a big hurry. So thanks a lot for the directions."

He took off running, dashing past the Lost Lizards of Los Angeles exhibition, the Spider Pavilion and the Gem and Mineral Hall. Breathless, he entered a large, darkened hall that was bordered on all sides by glass windows, behind which were lifelike scenes from typical early California life. Billy checked the big clock on the wall. He had used up five of his seventeen minutes and still hadn't made contact with Anacapa.

Quickly, his eyes scanned the dioramas. Each one represented a different era of California history. There was one showing some of the eleven families from Mexico that established the original pueblo of Los Angeles. There was another one that celebrated the discovery of oil in the area by showing a model of an oil drilling well. Ordinarily Billy might have been interested in stopping to watch the well pump, but he didn't have time to dawdle. He scanned the room quickly until his eyes fell on the diorama on the far wall. It showed the early California landscape with members of its earliest tribal inhabitants.

As he got closer, Billy was able to make out the figures inside the diorama. They were gathered around one of the round, thatched huts. Two men were kneeling by a log, digging out a canoe. A figure of a woman was crouched nearby. She was holding a baby in a willow carrier on her back while mashing acorns with a rounded stone. Off to one side, a hairy buffalo was grazing on the long, dry grasses, and next to him stood a beautiful Chumash girl wearing a cape made of animal skins. It was Anacapa.

Billy raced to the glass and pressed his face up close, waving to try to get her attention. But she was as still as a statue. In fact, she was a statue, as were all the other Chumash people in the scene.

"Anacapa," he said, rapping on the glass with his knuckles. "It's me. Billy Broccoli. The Hoove's friend. Remember me? We met yesterday on the playground. Well, we didn't actually meet. But I bet you remember me. . . I'm the bad dancer with two left feet."

The statue of Anacapa remained motionless.

"Hey," Billy said. "Are you listening? Can you hear me? If you can, give me some sign."

"I can hear you just fine," a little voice said.

It wasn't the kind of voice Billy assumed an Indian princess would have, but who was he to know what princesses should sound like. The only princess he knew was Breeze, and as far as he was concerned, she was only a princess in her own mind.

"Listen, Anacapa," he continued. "The Hoove sent me with a really important message for you."

"Who's the Hoove?" the little voice asked. "That's a funny name. Does he have diarrhea too?"

Billy knew that voice, and for sure, it was no princess. He whirled around to see Harry standing behind him, staring at him like he was wacko.

"You're a cuckoo bird," Harry said. "Don't you know those diorama people aren't real?"

"Listen up, Harry. I'm really busy here doing something very important that you could not possibly understand," Billy whispered, kneeling down to talk directly to the overly-curious little guy.

"Says you," Harry snapped back. "I

understand a lot of things, especially science stuff. Like I bet you don't know that the stegosaurus had a brain the size of a walnut."

"That's good to know, Harry. Really it is. Now go find a stegosaurus and have a conversation with it. The Dinosaur Hall isn't far away."

"But I want to stay and watch you talk to the statues again."

Harry's mum walked up to them and smiled.

"Oh, Harry. How nice that you've made a new friend," she said.

"Ma'am, I don't mean to be rude," Billy said urgently. "I'm sure Harry is a total blast to be with and everything, but I'm here on a school project and I've got to concentrate, so if you wouldn't mind. . ."

"Of course," she said. "Come on, Harry. Let's go visit the spider pavilion."

"No, Mummy. Spiders have venom and I don't like venom. I'm staying here."

"You're afraid of spiders?" Billy said with fake shock. "Spiders aren't scary. They can't hurt a tough kid like you. They are a garden's best friend."

"Says you," Harry said. "Did you know that a spider's venom turns the insides of their prey into liquid? I don't want to get turned into a liquid and be all gooey."

Billy looked at the clock on the wall. Ten minutes had elapsed, and Bennett would be there any second. He did not have time for long conversations with a budding science genius.

"I'm begging you," he said to Harry's mum. "My whole grade depends on this."

She nodded and took Harry's hand.

"Come on, sweetie," she said. "Let's go see the butterflies. Then we'll get some hot chocolate from the machine."

"Hot chocolate! Goody! See you later, Mr Cuckoo Bird," Harry said with a wave. As they turned to go, Billy heard him saying "Mummy, did you know that butterflies use their feet to taste?"

Relieved to be alone again, Billy turned back

to the glass and moved from side to side, trying to make eye contact with Anacapa, but her eyes looked lifeless and dull.

"Hey, Anacapa ... I'm over here," he said, tapping on the glass softly so as not to attract the attention of anyone else in the hall. "The Hoove told me to tell you that he couldn't make it here today. He had a problem with his leg. Or was it his hand? I forget, but that doesn't matter. The important thing is that he really wants to see you again and he's planning to come to our performance Friday night. You're coming to that, right?"

No answer.

"Of course you are," Billy went on. "You wouldn't let an important Chumash celebration happen without you. So you'll get to see the Hoove then, which is great because he's really counting on becoming friends with you. It's been a long time since he's had another ghost friend his age, and he thinks you're amazing."

The statue in the glass case didn't move. She

just stood there next to the hairy buffalo, looking like she was made of wax. From the corner of his eye, he saw Bennett striding across the hall, heading towards him. It was now or never.

"OK," he whispered to the glass. "I've got to go. The Hoove asked if you'd meet him tomorrow at noon. The cinema in the mall. Outside the doors of Screen Three. He said for me to tell you he can't wait to see you again because he has some big news to tell you, and he's sure you guys are going to be best friends, which is so important to him, because between you and me . . . and he doesn't like anyone to know this about him . . . but he's really lonely. It's been a long ninety-nine years."

Billy looked at Anacapa, studying her face for a sign that she had understood him.

"Anything?" he asked. "Did you hear anything that I said?"

Bennett was by his side now, placing a hand on his shoulder.

"Sorry it took so long to find a parking space," he said. "But I'm here now. Happy to share the few minutes we have remaining."

Billy tried to get Bennett to leave him alone in front of the diorama by suggesting that he needed time to really concentrate on the architecture of the thatched dwelling, but Bennett never left his side. He stared at every detail in the diorama, talking on and on about how the buffalo is the first cousin of the domestic cow. When that subject wound down, he moved right on to how you can tell that the buffalo is an herbivore because it has flat teeth to grind its food whereas meat eaters have sharp teeth to rip up their meat or kill their prey. Throughout the whole tooth lecture, Billy kept trying to get Anacapa's attention, but her eyes were unmoving.

After a few minutes, Bennett glanced at his watch.

"Hey, we have to go, Bill. I know it doesn't seem like seventeen minutes – time flies when you're talking about buffalo teeth. But I promised your mother I'd abide by her rules. And when Bennett Fielding makes a promise, you can take that to the bank."

Billy could see in Bennett's eyes that there was no choice. It was useless to argue. He sighed, then turned and followed his stepfather across the room, feeling that his mission had failed. How was he ever going to tell that to the Hoove, who was counting on him? As he craned his neck for one last backwards glance towards the diorama, an amazing thing happened. So amazing that it made his heart almost jump out of his body.

She blinked.

Yes, Anacapa blinked at him. There was no mistaking it. She had heard him, and answered.

Chapter 9

Billy assumed that when he arrived back home, he was going to find the Hoove exhausted from his busy day of doing good deeds, but instead, he found quite the opposite. The Hoove was full of energy, zipping around his room hanging up Billy's clothes and rearranging the socks in his sock drawer according to colour. When he saw Billy, he lunged at him, wanting to know everything that happened at the museum. He must have asked Billy at least a thousand questions about his encounter with Anacapa.

"Did she say she was excited about seeing me tomorrow?" he asked.

"Um . . . not exactly," Billy answered.

"Well, did she at least say that she was looking forward to going to the movies?"

"Um . . . not in so many words."

"But I'll bet she said that of all the ghosts she's met, I'm the coolest. At least tell me she said that, Billy Boy."

"Um . . . she didn't exactly say that," Billy said. "Actually, she was quiet. Very quiet. I mean, very very quiet."

"Yeah, I have that effect on the ladies. They see me, behold my good looks, and are stunned into silence. That's OK. I'll let her know that she doesn't have to be intimidated by my perfection."

"Hoove, maybe you shouldn't get your hopes up," Billy tried to say gently. "I mean, I think she's going to be there tomorrow at the mall, but you can never be entirely sure."

The Hoove shot Billy a suspicious look.

"Well, what exactly did she say?" he asked.

"It's an amazing thing about Anacapa. She says so much with so little."

"Billy Boy, will you stop making me play this

guessing game? Tell me the exact words she said."

"She spoke, but not with her mouth."

"Are you telling me she talks through her nose? That's weird, all right, but hey, I guess I could get used to it."

"No, Hoove. She spoke with her eyes. When I told her to meet you outside Screen Three at noon, she blinked."

"Blinked . . . you mean as in 'eyelids up and down'? That's it?"

"Yes . . . but it was a very meaningful blink. At least, I think it was."

"I'll take it," the Hoove said. "That's good enough for me. And now, moving on to the important part of my day tomorrow . . . my outfit. I have to dazzle those blinking eyes of hers."

The Hoove zipped inside Billy's wardobe and started rummaging around in his clothes, looking for something new to wear. He was thinking that maybe his shorts and tartan newsboy cap weren't the right look for a Native American princess. He spent the next two hours trying on everything in Billy's wardrobe. A baseball jersey. A T-shirt with a surfer on the back. A fleece gilet with a knit beanie. A navy blue suit with a red polka-dot tie. Checked Bermuda shorts with flip-flops. Finally, Billy convinced him to go with his original look, which had worked well for him for the last ninety-nine years. The Hoove agreed, probably because he had finally exhausted himself from his busy and nerve-wracking day.

As Billy settled down in bed that night, it occurred to him that the Hoove hadn't told him if he had heard from the Higher-Ups.

"Hey, Hoove," he whispered.

"Shhhh," the Hoove answered from the wardrobe. "I'm in the middle of my beauty rest."

"OK, just one question. Did you get the pass for Friday night from the Higher-Ups?"

"Not yet. I think maybe I took a few too many breaks today for them."

"You took breaks? On an important day like today? How many?"

"Somewhere between one and a hundred. But don't worry yourself about it. I'll fix things. I'm planning to get to the mall early tomorrow, and seal the deal."

"How?"

"Litter pick up," the Hoove said. "That's a deal closer if ever I heard of one. Once they see me tidying up in the halls and malls, those Higher-Ups will be so impressed, they will fall all over themselves to give me the pass."

"You're sure of that?"

"Yes. I feel it in my bones. At least, I would if I had bones. Now close your eyes and go off to dreamland. I have to get my beauty rest."

The next morning, the Hoove woke up early and wasted no time getting to the mall, arriving well before it opened. The car park was empty and the doors were locked up tight. But walls were not a problem for Hoover Porterhouse the Third. He floated by the parking structure and passed through the solid brick wall of the cinema wing until he found himself in the empty lobby. Determined to put his plan into effect right away, he looked around for some litter to clean up, but someone had beaten him to it. There wasn't so much as a kernel of popcorn on the carpet.

He floated down to Screen Three and stopped in front of the entrance, knowing that this was as far as his boundary would allow him to go. He peeked inside the theatre and saw the caretaker moving up and down the rows of seats, picking up popcorn boxes and sweet wrappers that people had thoughtlessly tossed on the floor the night before.

"Other beings might see a mess in here," the Hoove said to himself. "But not me. I see a mountain of brownie points."

He entered the semi-dark cinema and immediately zipped into action, grabbing a bin bag off the caretaker's cart and hypergliding up and down the rows. He scooped sweet wrappers and rubbish into his transparent arms at breakneck speed. The caretaker looked up, and from the corner of his eye, thought he saw an empty box of liquorice flying through the air, finding its way into the green bin bag.

"Man oh man," he said to himself. "I have to lay off the pepperoni pizza before bed. It's playing tricks with my mind."

The Hoove stood absolutely still until the caretaker was once again engaged in sweeping up the rubbish from under the seats into his dustbin. Then he turned his attention to picking up the fizzy drink cups and straws that had been left in the armrests, being careful to separate the plastic straws and lids so that they could be recycled.

"Check this out," he called out to the invisible Higher-Ups, who he hoped were observing him. "Not only am I cleaning up the cinema, I'm cleaning up the environment. If you ask me, that's definitely an extra credit kind of thing."

The cinema looked spotless in no time. Just

as the Hoove was about to leave, he noticed a man in a white shirt and tie come in and look around. He was obviously the manager.

"Excellent work, Clyde," the manager said to the caretaker. "You got this place looking tip-top in record time."

"I did?" Clyde said, very surprised to see the Hoove's overstuffed bin bags hanging off his cart. "I mean, yes, sir, I did."

"Come see me later," the manager said. "I'm very impressed with your work habits. I think perhaps it's time for us to talk about a promotion for you."

The caretaker's face lit up like fireworks on the fourth of July.

"Yes, sir," he said. "I could certainly use a promotion. I got two kids almost ready for university."

After the manager left, the caretaker pulled his phone out of his pocket and dialled a number.

"Anna," he said. "Anna, honey. You're not going to believe what just happened."

The Hoove smiled and pumped his fist.

"Talk about extra credit," he said, directing his voice skyward. "This little moment right here should be good enough to get me to any museum in the world."

The Hoove left the cinema feeling confident that he had done enough to earn his museum pass, so instead of continuing to do good deeds, he decided to take a little break. He floated down the mall to the video game store that was next to the doughnut stand, taking a few minutes to float above the doughnut case and just enjoy the aroma of the dark chocolate frosting. Then he went into the video game store to check out the displays. Unable to resist, he picked up one controller after another and played every game that was sitting on top of the counter. The minutes flew by. Maybe even an hour. He lost all track of time. The Hoove had never really understood all the fuss about video games, since when he was alive, they didn't exist. The most exciting game for kids then involved tossing horseshoes into a sand pit.

"Wow," he said to himself, his hands glued to a controller and his eyes to the screen. "This beats bobbing for apples any day."

The Hoove was so engrossed in one particular skateboarding game that he was totally caught off guard when the owner and his salesman opened up the shop and came bursting in.

"Hey," the owner yelled, noticing that all the TVs were on. "Is anyone in here?"

The Hoove stood very still and stopped playing. The men looked around suspiciously.

"You'd better call the electrician, Kevin," the owner said to his salesman. "We must have a short circuit somewhere. All the games seem to have turned on by themselves."

The Hoove put down the controller and floated away from the screen, laughing a little to himself.

"Call an electrician!" he sniggered. "People

always want to come up with some logical solution for what us ghosts do. I don't know why they can't just understand that we share the world with them."

Once outside the video game store, the Hoove glided around aimlessly for a while, trying to find something to amuse himself. Eventually, though, he looked up at the large clock above the doughnut stand. It was actually shaped like a doughnut, and the hands looked like they were decorated with chocolate sprinkles. It was exactly five to twelve, time to go meet Anacapa. He considered dipping behind the counter and taking a doughnut for her. As a ghost, she couldn't eat, but she might enjoy the sweet smell. Then he thought better of it. Billy had told him that the Chumash ate ground acorns and nuts, so she probably wouldn't appreciate a maple glazed doughnut with jelly filling. Not to mention the fact that the Higher-Ups would definitely not appreciate him swiping a doughnut without paying for it.

The Hoove hurried down the hall to the cinema entrance, taking a minute or two to spin around the turnstile in a series of flying somersaults. He didn't like to admit it, but he was suddenly feeling pretty anxious about meeting Anacapa, and the somersaults helped him release some of his nervous energy.

He passed through the cinema lobby and went to the entrance to Screen Three – of course, being careful not to cross the line into Screens Four through Nine. And then he waited.

And waited.

And waited.

Noon came and went, but Anacapa didn't show up. Twelve fifteen came and went, but still no Anacapa. By twelve thirty, the Hoove was doing his version of pacing, zooming back and forth so fast that it created an unpleasant breeze for the moviegoers. Several of them asked the manager if he could turn down the air conditioning. By twelve forty-five, the Hoove was so upset that he was emitting a tart orange smell, even more pungent than usual. He hadn't admitted to himself how important this meeting with Anacapa was. He was really counting on getting to know her as a ghost friend, and the thought that she wasn't showing up made him incredibly sad.

He waited until two o'clock before he finally made the difficult decision to leave. With one last look around to make sure Anacapa wasn't hiding somewhere in the lobby, he sighed deeply and floated slowly out of the cinema into the mall. The smell of the chocolate doughnuts wafted towards him, but it was no longer pleasing to him. The noise of the video games didn't sound fun any more – they were nothing but annoying bleeps and peeps.

The Hoove left the mall, passing through the brick wall behind the cinema, and paused outside in the sunlight. He hoped the fresh air and warm California weather would cheer him up. That didn't work, but something else did.

"Hoover!" he heard a breathless voice call. "Hoover Porterhouse the Third!"

He looked up, and there, hovering in the air above him, was Anacapa, her straight black hair and deerskin cape blowing in the breeze.

"Oh, look who decided to show up," he said. "I guess being on time is not a Chumash tradition."

"I'm so sorry," she said, floating down to be at eye level with him. "You have every right to be angry. But I hope my explanation will help you understand why I'm so late."

"All right. I'll listen with one ear and give you two minutes."

"I was called into action very suddenly," she said. "A brown pelican was in distress."

"A pelican? As in those birds whose mouth can hold more than their belly-can?"

Anacapa giggled.

"That is very clever," she said.

"The truth be known, I didn't make that up. I heard it in a poem once."

"Oh, you read poetry?"

"Me? I eat poetry for breakfast. So what about this pelican? You got my curiosity going."

"It was awful, Hoover. The poor bird had got caught in those plastic rings that hold six-packs of fizzy-drink cans together. He was floating in the ocean, completely entangled, and the plastic was around his beak, so he wasn't able to catch fish or eat."

"I didn't know birds drank fizzy drinks."

"They don't. People leave their plastic rubbish on the beach and it gets pulled into the water and floats all over the world. Did you know that there is something called the Great Pacific Garbage Patch that's a huge island made up of plastic that floats in the ocean for ever?"

"And your job is to get rid of these plastic rings?"

"My job is to protect the land and the oceans, like my people did. The pelican needed my help. I had no choice but to go."

"So you flew in like Superwoman and saved him?"

Anacapa giggled again.

"I don't know this Superwoman you speak of," she said. "But she sounds very powerful."

The Hoove took a minute to ponder everything that Anacapa had just told him. He had never been a huge fan of the bird world. The birds he knew were often messengers from the Higher-Ups. All their squawking and wing flapping rattled his nerves. He preferred animals of the cat family, like lions and tigers. He loved the way they crept around on graceful feet, their eyes darting everywhere. But still, birds had a right to live, free from getting caught in the trappings of modern human life.

"So, like, in bird society, you're a pretty big deal?" he asked.

"I love all land and sea creatures," she told him. "Last week I helped save a sea lion who was caught in a fishing net. I set him free and he swam away to rejoin his family."

"Wait," the Hoove said, his ears perking up at the word *lion*. "Are you telling me that lions swim in the ocean?"

"No, silly," Anacapa laughed. "The California sea lion is like a seal, with ears. They're very intelligent."

"Yeah, I knew that," the Hoove said, even though he didn't. "I'm very partial to lions. I think it's super cool to save them, the kind that live in the sea. You can be late for me anytime doing that kind of stuff. Anyway, the important thing is that we have some time now to get to know each other."

"Oh, I am so sorry, Hoover," Anacapa said. "Actually, I have to go back to the beach to see how the bird is doing, so I can't stay. But why don't you come with me?"

"That's a great idea. But . . . um. . ."

The Hoove hesitated. The last thing he wanted to tell Anacapa was that he couldn't go with her because he was grounded for being an irresponsible ghost. She was the opposite of irresponsible. She was a hero, flying around California saving birds and sea lions and the land itself. And how had he spent his morning? Playing video games in the mall and sniffing chocolate doughnuts.

"Come on, Hoover," she was saying. "We just have to fly over the mountains and we will be at the Santa Monica Beach. We can be there in five minutes if you know how to hyperglide."

"Yeah, well, that's exactly the problem," the Hoove said, relieved that she had given him an excuse. "My hyperglide mechanism is temporarily in the shop. The Higher-Ups are making some adjustments on the hyper part. Or maybe it's the glide part. In any case, I have to take a pass on the beach trip."

"So then I won't see you tonight, either?" Anacapa asked. "Your friend Billy said you were coming to the Native American Night celebration at the museum."

"Oh, I am. I'm just coming slowly."

"Good, because it is going to be a wonderful

night, full of people learning about my culture. And Billy has finally learned his dance. He has a right and a left foot now."

"This I got to see."

"Good," Anacapa said, flashing Hoover her beautiful glowing smile. "We can enjoy the celebration together, then. It will be a wonderful way for you to get to know me and what is important to me. That is what true friendship is based on."

"I couldn't agree more."

"Then I will see you tonight at seven. At the museum. I will be waiting for you in the diorama, in my place next to the hairy buffalo. Do you promise me you will be there?"

"Do I promise?" the Hoove said. "Does a zebra have stripes? Does an elephant have a trunk? Is water wet? Does a fire have flames?"

Anacapa laughed. The sound of her laughter mingled with the wind and flew in and out of the Hoove's ears, making him very dizzy, in a good kind of way.

"I understand from what you are saying," she said, "that the answer is yes."

"You can make that yes with a capital *Y*," the Hoove answered. "I promise."

"Until tonight, then, Hoover Porterhouse the Third."

She smiled at him, and then spiralled into the air so quickly that all he could see was the fringe on her animal–skin cape as it sailed westward to the ocean.

After Anacapa left, the Hoove felt like a new person. He was positively bursting with anticipation about the celebration that night. He would watch Billy dance, and enjoy seeing all the Chumash crafts and foods. And most of all, he and Anacapa would laugh together like best friends do.

He turned up to the sky and called out.

"OK, guys. The time has come. I have proven myself a worthy and responsible ghost. Now it's your turn to deliver. Can I go to the museum tonight? I'm waiting to hear that big YES."

There was no answer from above.

"Perhaps you didn't hear me," he called, "so let me re-utter the question."

Before he could get the words out of his mouth, the door to the mall swung open and Clyde came out, pushing his caretaker's cart. As he passed by the Hoove, one of the green bin bags opened up and an empty box of popcorn fell out at his feet. The Hoove reached down and picked it up, inspecting the butter stains on the inside.

It couldn't be true, but it was.

As he stared at those buttery marks, the Hoove realized that the trail they left on the cardboard spelled out a word.

And that word was *NO*.

Chapter 10

By six o'clock that night, Billy had got himself into a state of panic. He was rushing around his room, filled with excitement about the performance that was now only an hour away. The Hoove was the exact opposite of excited. He was miserable and feeling very sorry for himself.

"Hoove," Billy said. "Have you seen my two eagle feathers? I remember putting them right here on my desk."

"Perhaps they flew away," he answered grimly. "They're probably looking for the eagle tail they fell out of."

Billy put on the beige T-shirt that he and Ruby had each decided to wear, and looked at himself in the mirror.

"Hey, Hoove, does this beige shirt actually look like skin? It's supposed to."

The Hoove didn't even look up. He was flopped on the bed, lying face down.

"The Chumash men danced bare chested," Billy went on, "but when you have a chest like mine, which curves in instead of out, you're not exactly wild about letting everyone see it. You know what I mean?"

The Hoove picked up his head just enough to study Billy in his beige shirt.

"Let me just say this. If you're going for the Chinese hairless dog look, you've got it down."

Billy finished tucking his shirt into his beige pants, which were also supposed to look like skin, then turned around to face the Hoove.

"Listen, Hoove," he said. "You're my buddy, and I'm really sorry you can't come tonight. Believe me, I wish you could be there. Is there anything you want me to tell Anacapa?"

"Yeah, tell her it was nice knowing her."

"You'll see her again, Hoove. This isn't your last chance."

"Listen, Billy Boy. I've been around a lot longer than you. And as an observer of the human being, this is what I know for sure. Female humans do not take kindly to people who don't keep their word. Especially this particular Chumash princess. She flies all over southern California saving little birdies, big birdies, even lions that swim in the sea. She is a serious person who keeps her serious promises. And here I am, flaking out on my promise to her for the second time. That does not bode well for a long-standing friendship."

"Don't you think she'd understand, Hoove?"

"Yeah, she'd understand all right. That she can't count on Hoover Porterhouse the Third."

There was a knock on the door of Billy's room.

"I'm coming!" Billy called. "Be right there."

"Get a move on, Chief Yellow Snow," Breeze yelled from the other side of the door. "Mum says we have to get in the car now. Bennett is

150

already hysterical about not being able to find a good parking space."

"Two more seconds, Breeze. I'm just putting some eagle feathers into my hair."

"Tell me I didn't hear that," Breeze muttered to herself as she trotted back down the hall.

Even though he was excited for the evening, Billy was finding it hard to leave the Hoove behind. The Hoove wasn't even able to put up a brave front. He looked so sad and dejected, stretched out on Billy's bed like a lifeless blob. Billy put a few more things into his rucksack, and hesitated before opening the door to go join his family.

"It's not fair, is it, Hoove?" he said quietly. "That you can't go."

"Fair isn't even in the neighbourhood, my friend. I did every good deed I could think of, and then some. Carried groceries, picked up rubbish, washed the car. I even helped a man get promoted. What more can a guy do to get their approval?"

Billy didn't have an answer, but the Hoove did.

"I could make stuff up. I could promise them that I'm going to devote my life to working with Bennett to discover a cure for tooth decay."

"Except that you don't know the first thing about teeth," Billy pointed out.

"Well then, I could promise to single-handedly remove every piece of used chewing gum from underneath school desks. How's that for an idea?"

"Hoove, stop." Billy held up his hand so the Hoove would stop talking and listen for once. "There's something else you could do, and it's really simple."

"Please, Mr All-Knowing. Enlighten me."

"You could tell the Higher-Ups the truth," Billy said. "Just the plain, simple truth."

"I'm not following you, Billy Boy."

"That you're lonely here and that you really want to make a friend."

"That is a very embarrassing thing to admit,

Billy Boy. Hoover Porterhouse does not play that way."

"I know you think that way, Hoove. But let me tell you what happened with Ruby. You told me not to tell her the truth, to pretend that I was a great dancer and all full of confidence and charm and stuff. When I did that, all that happened was that I stomped all over her feet. When I finally confessed that I had two left feet and was totally embarrassed about it, she understood and helped me learn the dance. Telling her the truth worked."

Suddenly, the door to Billy's room burst open and his mother's head appeared.

"Who are you talking to, honey?" she asked.

"Uh . . . just rehearsing my lines for tonight, Mum."

"Oh, I didn't know you had a speaking part."

"I don't, but just in case they call on me to explain exactly how fine the Chumash ground their acorns, I want to be ready."

Billy's mum looked a little puzzled. It wasn't the first time her son had offered up a strange explanation for his behaviour. But there wasn't time to get into that. They had motorways to drive, a parking space to find and a performance to attend.

"Come along right now," she said to Billy. "Bennett and Breeze are already in the car. I'll grab your rucksack."

Billy glanced back at the Hoove, who was floating above the bed now and gazing sadly out the window at the car in the drive.

"Give it your best shot," Billy whispered to him.

"Honestly, honey," Billy's mum said. "Carrying a rucksack isn't that hard. I don't think I need to give it my best shot."

And she was out of the door, with Billy following close behind.

That left the Hoove alone, all alone. For the first time in his life as a ghost, he felt defeated. He was out of ideas, out of clever plans, out of complicated schemes. The only one left was Billy's. Tell the truth.

"Give it your best shot," he repeated to himself. "OK, Billy Boy, here goes nothing."

He took off his tartan cap, rolled it up and stuffed it in the back pocket of his shorts. Straightening his hair and adjusting his suspenders, he floated to the middle of the room, took a breath, looked skyward, and began to speak.

"OK, Mr Higher-Ups. Or maybe there's some Ms Higher-Ups also. Anyway, whoever you are, I need you to hear me now. I have been trying to be what you want me to be for ninety-nine years. And in both life years and ghost years, that's a loooong time. And the thing is, I never get your complete approval, even though I'm trying my best down here. What is it with you guys . . . or gals?"

He waited for an answer but none came.

"It's like you expect me to be perfect," he went on, "but I'm here to tell you, there is no such thing as perfection. Well, I come close, I must admit."

The Hoove stopped to enjoy his little joke, until he realized he was laughing alone.

"Seriously, folks, it's lonely down here. Sure, you sent me to Billy, and he's a really good guy. But he's human. He's going to grow up. Go to high school. Get a date for prom. Go to university and live in a dorm with lots of other kids. Move out of this house, leaving me here surrounded by the same four walls because I never seem to get it right. And now I'm not asking for that much. I have a chance to make a friend, who's a ghost like me. Who can be my friend for all eternity. And what do you do?"

Again, he waited for an answer. And again, none came.

"I'll tell you what you do. You block me at every turn. I know that sometimes I mess up. I don't finish a task or do everything that I promised to do. But I'm asking you to look at the whole me, the me that is trying to be the best ghost I can be. And if you do, you will see that I have earned the right to go to the museum for one night. Is that asking so much?"

The Hoove stood there with his transparent arms outstretched and waited for a sign.

"Come on," he pleaded. "I meant what I said. Give a guy a break!"

He glanced around for a sign, any sign. But all he saw was the twilight as it came through the window and silently cast a soft purple glow over Billy's room.

Chapter 11

By the time Billy and his family arrived at the Natural History Museum, it was swarming with people. All the middle school parents had turned out to watch their kids perform in the Native American Night celebration. The old grey-haired guard stood outside of the front door, waving his arms like a windmill in a hurricane, desperately trying to direct the cluster of parents who were competing for the best parking spaces.

The Broccoli-Fieldings sat in their car, impatiently waiting to get into the car park. Billy's mum was wringing her hands nervously.

"I'm supposed to introduce the evening," she said. "It simply won't do for me to be the last one to arrive. Billy, I wish you hadn't taken so long to get ready. Now we're going to be late."

"The youngster had a lot to do," Breeze said. "It takes time to stand in your room talking to yourself. You don't want to rush a thing like that."

"I was not talking to myself," Billy insisted. "I was talking to my hair, trying to get it to cooperate with the eagle feathers."

"That is so weird, I'd actually prefer that you had been talking to yourself," Breeze said. "It's way less crazy."

Luckily, Bennett's very sharp vision (perfected from years of looking into the small crevices of his patients' teeth) allowed him to spot a woman hurrying to her car several spaces behind them.

"I'm going to get that space," he said excitedly. "I just have to back up a little so she can pull out."

Bennett put the car in reverse and was just about to back up, when there was a tapping on his driver's side window. He rolled the window down and a huge buffalo head with two angry horns poked its way into the car.

"You're in violation of Division 11, Section 23109.2, of the California Vehicle Code," the buffalo face said. "Driving in reverse in heavy traffic. I'm going to have to issue you a citation."

"Rod," Billy called out from the back seat. "Get your horns out of our car and go find your herd."

Rod lifted up the flap on his buffalo mask to reveal his sweaty face.

"How'd you know it was me?"

"Maybe because you're the only buffalo on the planet who knows the California Vehicle Code by heart," Breeze said.

"You got a point." Rod nodded. "Nevertheless, Dr Fielding, I'm going to have to write you up."

"Rod, we're due inside immediately," Mrs Broccoli-Fielding said, using her head teacher's voice to make it perfectly clear that this conversation was not going to continue. "You certainly don't want anyone to miss seeing that buffalo mask you must have worked very hard on. Bennett, I'll take the children inside while you park." Then, lowering her voice, she added, "In that primo space right behind us."

"Where will I meet you?" Bennett asked while his wife was ushering Billy and Breeze out of the car.

"In the California Hall of History where the dioramas are," Billy called out to him. "Right next to the hairy buffalo." Then, looking over at Rod, he added, "And I'm not referring to you."

"Hey, I'm as hairy as any other buffalo," Rod complained.

But no one was listening. Billy and Breeze, led by Mrs Bennett-Fielding, were hurrying up the steps and into the museum. By the time they got to the California Hall of History, most of the parents were already seated in the rows of plastic folding chairs the museum staff had put out for the performance. The chairs were placed in a semi-circle near the Chumash diorama, creating a stage area right in front of it. The glass windows that covered the diorama had been pulled aside so that the audience could get a clear view of the Chumash village and see the statues of the men digging out their canoe and the woman mashing acorns with her baby on her back. Off to one side, the hairy buffalo stood grazing amidst the long grasses, and next to him a motionless Anacapa appeared, as still as a wax figure.

While Billy's mum rushed up to the podium to prepare for her introductory remarks, Billy wandered over to Anacapa and stared intently into her face.

"Can you hear me?" he whispered.

"Yes, Billy, I can," said a voice right behind him. He wheeled around to see Ruby Baker smiling at him. She was wearing her matching beige T-shirt and eagle feathers in her hair.

"Oh, Ruby. I didn't know you were here."

"You didn't? Then who were you talking to?"

Billy hesitated. He couldn't use the old "*I'm just rehearsing my lines*" excuse with Ruby, because she knew he didn't have any lines. Fortunately, though, he didn't have to come up with any explanation at all, because their conversation was interrupted by Mr Wallwetter approaching them. He was wearing a large, feathered Native American war bonnet. Because his head was too small for his body, it looked like an overweight peacock had landed on top of him.

"I've been asked to have the whole class sit down in front of the stage area," Mr Wallwetter said. "After the head teacher's introduction, we will begin with the oral presentations, followed by the basket weaving and archery demonstrations. Our grand finale will be the music and dance portion of the show."

"Come on, Billy," Ruby said. "Let's sit together."

"Why don't you save me a place, Ruby. I'll be right there. I just want to take another minute to study the diorama."

"Wow, Billy. I'm so impressed with how

seriously you're taking this whole Native American Night."

"If only Billy took learning his punctuation marks half as seriously," Mr Wallwetter said. "His use of the semicolon leaves much to be desired."

Billy couldn't stop himself from letting out a little groan. Even with a peacock on his head, Mr Wallwetter was just was not capable of lightening up. He just stood there wearing his sourpuss semicolon face and waiting for Billy to answer.

"Actually, Mr Wallwetter," Billy said, "I know this will come as a shock to you, but I don't enjoy punctuation all that much. I find that semicolons and I don't have much in common. However, I do love studying the Chumash people. It's almost like they're alive to me."

As he said that, Billy glanced over at Anacapa. He was sure he saw her smile.

Ruby followed grumpy Mr Wallwetter over to the area where the students were taking their seats, leaving Billy facing Anacapa. The minute they were alone, she spoke.

"Where is he?" she asked, barely moving her lips.

"Who?" Billy tried to pretend he had no idea whom she was talking about.

"You know who. He promised he'd be here. He said yes with a capital *Y*."

Billy winced. He didn't want to tell her that the Hoove wasn't coming.

"I'm sure he's trying his best to get here," was all he could muster.

"Oh, this makes me so angry," Anacapa said. "He gave me his word and now he's broken it again! He is so irresponsible."

There it was, that word again. *Irresponsible.* It seemed to follow the Hoove around like his shadow on a sunny day.

"Anacapa, he tries to be responsible, he really does. He's just got some ... um ... special circumstances to deal with," Billy tried to explain.

"He is no more special than anyone else," she said, anger shooting out of her dark, intense eyes. "He just thinks he is. Well, he can't treat me like this. A promise is a promise. A good person keeps his word."

Suddenly, her full body materialized from the statue and a transparent Anacapa . . . the spirit of Anacapa . . . shot into the air and began to fly furiously around the darkened hall. She circled the room in huge angry circles, her words echoing in Billy's ears. "A good person keeps his word. A good person keeps his word."

Although Billy could understand her feelings, it was still scary to see her acting out her fury. He looked around to see if anyone else noticed her zooming above them. Her statue in the diorama remained still and lifeless, as it always did. Her spirit was visible only to him.

"Hey, Broccoli, they sent me over here to get you," Rod Brownstone said, tapping Billy hard on the shoulder. "Wallwetter's getting pretty hot under the collar."

"He's not the only one," Billy muttered, as he watched Anacapa zoom angrily around the room.

Billy felt a cold breeze whoosh by him, and he turned to see Anacapa coming in for a landing. She zoomed into the diorama and lighted on top of the hairy buffalo facing him.

"You tell your friend Hoover that any friendship between us is no longer possible," she said. "Friends don't lie to each other."

Anacapa formed both her hands into fists and pounded on the buffalo's hairy head. To Billy's utter shock, the buffalo let out a groan and snorted. Was he a ghost, too?

"Hey, did that buffalo just snort?" he found himself saying before he could stop himself.

Rod Brownstone lifted the flap on his buffalo mask and stared at him like his brains had turned to marshmallow sauce.

"You know what, Broccoli? You're strange. You see and hear things normal people don't. I don't know what's going on with you, but one day, I'll find out. You're on my radar, Cheese Sauce, and don't ever forget it."

"You must go now, Billy," Anacapa said, "and take this unpleasant buffalo boy away from me. Go join in the Chumash celebration. I will calm myself down and be with you to guide your feet."

Billy hurried over to the stage area and s at down, just as his mother was giving her introductory remarks. She thanked the museum for letting them hold their Native American celebration there. She thanked the students for working so hard on their projects. She thanked the teachers for going beyond the call of duty to teach the students the Chumash ways. She thanked the parents for showing up to support their kids. She thanked the three or four tribal members who had come to the museum to support the celebration. She thanked the artist who painted the diorama murals and the taxidermist who stuffed the animals in the displays. She thanked the guard for directing traffic and the audiovisual staff for hooking up her microphone. She even thanked the caretakers for restocking all the paper towels in the bathrooms.

"Your mum sure is polite," Ruby whispered in Billy's ear.

"And long-winded," Rod commented into Billy's other ear. Even though he was wearing the buffalo mask, Billy could still catch a whiff of Rod's breath, which smelled like an elderly fish had taken up residence in his mouth.

To be honest, Billy himself wondered why his mum was going on so long. She usually gave quick, cute little speeches. Then he realized that she was stalling, waiting for Bennett to arrive. The moment Bennett came rushing into the hall, she wrapped up the thank-yous and got on with the show. That was just like his mum to wait for Bennett. She always wanted to be sure everyone was included.

"Ladies and gentlemen," she said, abruptly ending the parade of thank-yous. "I now ask you to travel with me hundreds of years into the past, when the Chumash were the only people living in and preserving this beautiful land we now call California."

And with that, the show was on.

A group of seventh graders recited fascinating details about the Chumash tribe, like the fact that the average Chumash person ate three hundred pounds of acorns a year. Then there was a Chumash fashion show where several girls modelled capes and skirts made of pretend animal hide, and Billy's friend Ricardo modelled a headdress made of woodpecker feathers. Kayla Weeks demonstrated how the tribal women used rocks to grind acorns into flour. When she had trouble getting the acorn to break into small pieces, Anacapa floated over to her and guided her hands in the proper motion. Billy studied Kayla's face carefully to see if she felt Anacapa's presence, but he saw nothing except Kayla's happy smile and mass of red curls bobbing up and down.

The bow and arrow demonstrations followed,

and then the entire seventh grade sang a Chumash song, while a group of kids from the school jazz band beat out a rhythm with long sticks. Anacapa sang along, and although none of the audience could hear her, Billy recognized her beautiful, lilting voice.

It was almost eight o'clock by the time they were ready for the final dance number. Louise Niles, herself wearing moccasins and a beaded headband, introduced all ten couples who were going to perform.

"Good luck to us," Ruby whispered to Billy as they joined the others on the stage.

All the kids formed a circle directly in front of the diorama. Fortunately (or unfortunately, depending on how you look at it), Billy and Ruby were placed in the front of the circle, where everyone in the audience could see them the best.

"I hope I don't mess up," Billy whispered to Ruby. His hands were sweaty and his mouth was dry as cotton.

"Trust me, you will," Rod Brownstone whispered back, lifting the flap on his buffalo mask. He and Michelle Dines were the couple next to Billy and Ruby.

Ruby was busy waving to her parents and grinning into the camera they were holding up, so she didn't hear Billy talking. But Anacapa did. She floated over to Billy and hovered above his head.

"Do not worry," she whispered into his ear. "I am with you. I will guide your feet."

The drumming began and Billy took a deep breath. He felt like all eyes in the great hall were focused on him. The dance began slowly, and Billy concentrated on his feet, counting out the rhythm of the steps as he had practised. He crouched low and turned in a circle. Reaching out to take Ruby's hand at just the right moment, they circled each other, shifting their weight from foot to foot.

It was working. They were actually dancing!

But as the music sped up, Billy struggled to

keep up with the beat. His steps became unsteady and he felt like he was teetering, about to fall down.

Oh no, he thought. *Not here. Not now.*

"I am with you," he heard Anacapa say.

And then he felt her strong hands pulling him upright and guiding his feet in time to the music. He knew there was no way she would let him fall. Being supported like that was a great feeling, and gave Billy confidence to throw himself fully into the spirit of the dance. He listened to the drumming and began to feel the rhythm lifting his body and spirits. Letting out a spontaneous whoop, he started to spin in a circle, picking up speed as the drumming grew more intense. He felt like he and the music were one – that his feet, once so clumsy, were floating inches above the ground.

"Whoa, look at that boy go!" A ghostly voice sounded throughout the great hall, echoing off the domed roof. "I tell you, Billy Boy, your feet are on fire! You are doing the Hoove proud."

Billy looked up and was shocked to see the Hoove, flying across the hall in his fastest hyperglide mode.

"It worked!" the Hoove called out. "I told them the truth and got a twenty-four-hour pass. Here I am in all my glory!"

The Hoove spun in mid-air and did a series of fancy somersaults beneath the dome. At that exact moment, Anacapa looked up from the dance and saw him, too.

"Hey, Princess!" The Hoove grinned down at her with a cocky wave of his cap. "I bet you're glad to see me!"

Anacapa wasn't at all glad to see him. In fact, she was furious. She was so angry, she let go of Billy and flew up to the ceiling to confront him.

"How dare you come this late?" she said. "You've missed the whole celebration that I worked so hard on. And most of Billy's dance, too! You call yourself a friend? Some friend!"

Meanwhile, down on the ground, without Anacapa to hold him up, Billy had spun out of control. Dizzy from dancing in a circle, he spun wildly around, eventually losing his balance and crashing into the other dancing couples. He reached out for anything to stop him from falling, and found himself grabbing for Rod Brownstone's buffalo horns.

"Let go of my horns," Brownstone yelled at him. "They're only papier-mâché. You're going to pull them off."

It was too late. As he headed for the floor, Billy clutched the left horn, and with one final wild spin, yanked it off. Still holding it, he tumbled to the ground, where he rolled smack into the middle of the diorama and collapsed at the feet of the hairy buffalo. The buffalo looked down at Billy holding a horn that looked very much like his own. Billy thought he heard the buffalo let out a nasty snort and saw him paw the ground aggressively with his cloven hoof.

It all happened so fast, he couldn't be sure. Was he about to be attacked by the ghost of a hairy buffalo? No, it couldn't be. Or could it? The buffalo's nostrils were definitely flaring.

"I don't suppose you want to dance," Billy said to the buffalo, trying to lighten the situation up with a weak joke.

Again, he heard an angry snort and thought he saw the buffalo's eyes move. Then Anacapa swept into the diorama. Her statue remained unchanged . . . it was only her spirit that flew in to save him.

"Calm down, oh noble buffalo spirit," she said, placing herself between Billy and the buffalo. "This human boy means no harm. He is our friend."

Instantly, the snorting disappeared and the buffalo became perfectly still, a peaceful expression overtaking his waxen face. Billy breathed a sigh of relief.

As his focus returned, the realization hit him that he was sprawled out on the floor of the diorama, and that the entire audience was howling with laughter at the sight of him. He felt his face turn bright red and the tips of his ears grow hot with embarrassment.

"I will help you to your feet," Anacapa whispered to him.

"Stand up and take a bow," he heard the Hoove call. "Make it look like you planned it."

But Billy was too embarrassed and stunned to do anything but try to muster a sheepish grin. Rod Brownstone seized the moment to rub it in. He pulled off his mask and faced the crowd.

"This comedy event was brought to you by none other than Billy Broccoli," he proclaimed. "Let's all hear it for our own Chumash Clown."

"Oh, no you don't," the Hoove called out. "Nobody makes fun of Billy as long as I'm around."

Faster than you could say, "Rod Brownstone is a bully", the Hoove swept into the diorama and stood behind Rod, assuming his prime wedgie position. To the surprise of the audience, suddenly the smug Mr Brownstone broke into a vigorous dance, but it wasn't a dance of the

Chumash variety. It was the kind of dance you do when someone is giving you the biggest wedgie of your life.

"No one talks about my friend that way," Hoover Porterhouse the Third said as he tugged on Rod's jeans. Even Billy had to laugh.

"Hey, do I know how to be a good friend or not?" The Hoove grinned, aiming his pointed remark directly at Anacapa.

He flashed her his most charming smile.

"Not," she said, definitely not returning his smile.

And without another word, she left the diorama, flew up to the ceiling, and disappeared through the dome, bolting speedily into the night sky.

Chapter 12

After the performance, Billy and Breeze sat on the museum steps waiting for their parents to come out.

"I'm never going to live this down," Billy moaned. "I looked like a complete jerk up there."

"Hey, it wasn't a total disaster," Breeze said. "After all, you got a chance to dance with a hairy buffalo. How many guys can say that?"

"None. And I wish I was one of them."

Breeze's phone rang. She didn't jump to get it like she always did.

"If you want, I can just sit here with you," she said softly to Billy. "Maybe I can come up with some comforting big-sister kind of stuff to say, like 'you know, nobody's even going to remember this tomorrow.' That kind of stuff."

Billy smiled. Breeze was doing her best to protect him. They had been brother and sister for a few months, and it felt very good. As he took a deep breath to try to let go of the tension of the evening, he became aware of the tart smell of oranges in the air. And sure enough, there was Hoover Porterhouse coming in for a landing.

"Billy Boy, we got to talk," he said. "It's urgent."

Billy turned to Breeze. "Why don't you go see what's taking Mum and your dad so long?" he said to her. "I'm OK out here."

"You sure, little brother?"

"Yup," Billy said. "And Breeze, thanks."

The minute she got up and headed towards the steps to the museum, the Hoove began to talk.

"Where is Anacapa?" he asked.

"You tell me, Hoove."

"That's just it. I don't know. I've been looking for her all over the place. I've been in every room of this museum, including the Spider Pavilion, which, if I do say so myself, took a lot of guts because I am not partial to eight-legged bugs that bite."

"They're not bugs, Hoove. They're arachnids."

"Fine. Call them whatever fancy name you like. I just don't want them crawling up my leg . . . or lack of same. The point is, Anacapa is gone. Disappeared. Vamoosed."

"She probably just doesn't want to see you. She was pretty angry that you broke your promise again."

The Hoove let out a sigh of frustration.

"I tried to keep my promise, I really did," he said. "I did what you said . . . confessed everything to the Higher-Ups. And you know what? It worked. The minute they appeared and gave me that pass, I was out of there. I came as fast as I could."

"She doesn't know that. All she knows is that

you were an hour late and missed most of the celebration you had promised to attend."

"So what was I supposed to do? Tell her that I've been grounded for ninety-nine years and that I keep getting grounded because I just can't get it right? Let's face it, Billy. I'm nothing but a big flop as a ghost. Look at tonight: I even caused you to screw up your dance. I can't keep from messing up, no matter how much I care or how hard I try. Who would want a guy like me for a friend? Especially for all eternity?"

As soon as the Hoove finished speaking, a soft breeze that seemed to come from nowhere blew in and picked up a few leaves that were lying on the steps. Billy watched as the leaves rose into the air and slowly, gently took on a human shape in front of his eyes. In a poof of pink light, the shape became Anacapa.

"I heard everything you just said, Hoover," she said. There was no sign of anger in her voice now.

The Hoove looked totally flustered.

"So, like ... you mean ... everything ... including the 'grounded' part and the 'messing up' part and all?" he stammered.

She nodded.

"Why didn't you just tell me the truth in the first place?" she asked.

The Hoove looked from her to Billy, who shrugged as if to say, I told you so.

"That seems to be the question of the day," he said. "Billy Boy here is also a big fan of telling the truth. I guess I was embarrassed."

"About what?"

"I don't know. I just didn't want you to think of me as a bad guy. You're so good and do such important things. And what am I? True, I'm a good-looking ghost with a lot of personality, but what else am I?"

"Why don't we start over and I can find out," Anacapa said. "You said you have a twenty-four-hour pass. Come with me and you can tell me all about yourself. The real you."

A big smile crept across Billy's face. He liked

the way this was turning out for the Hoove. But he was totally surprised at the Hoove's answer.

"I'd like to come with you," he said to Anacapa. "But my pal Billy here is feeling pretty down in the dumps. I need to stay here with him and cheer him up."

"Those aren't the words of a bad guy," Anacapa said. "Those are the words of a very nice guy."

"Wait," Billy said, standing up suddenly. "I'm OK, Hoove. Really I am." He couldn't believe that the Hoove was willing to give up his time with Anacapa to be with him.

"You should go with Anacapa," he added.

"Who's Anacapa?" Breeze asked. She had just come out of the museum with Billy's mum and Bennett and Dr Marion Russo, the director of the museum.

"Uh . . . Anacapa?" Billy stammered. "Did I say Anacapa?" Once again, he was at a loss for an explanation.

"Anacapa," said Dr Russo, "is one of the

Channel Islands off the coast of Southern California. The word comes from the Chumash language, meaning 'Mirage Island'."

"That's how I got my name," Anacapa said to the Hoove. "I appear and disappear, like a mirage."

"You have obviously studied well for this night, Billy," Dr Russo continued. "I hope you found your experience worthwhile."

"Well, it's certainly had its ups and downs," Billy said, pleased that he could offer a little joke at his own expense.

"I think Bill handled himself quite well under the circumstances," Bennett agreed. "Always remember, Bill. It's not how many times you fall down that counts. It's how many times you get up."

"Now that," said the Hoove, turning to Anacapa, "is the first thing this guy has ever said that makes sense."

"I think our family should go out for pizza to celebrate Billy's falling down and getting up,"

Billy's mum said, putting her arm around Billy. "You've been grounded long enough. Would you like that, honey?"

Billy looked over at the Hoove, as if to ask his permission to go.

"Hey," the Hoove said. "Hoove's Rule Number Three. Never say no to pizza."

Billy flashed him a little thumbs-up, then headed down the steps with his family.

The Hoove turned to Anacapa.

"So, it looks like you're stuck with me," he said. "If you still want to hang out."

"Let's fly," she said. "I'll show you my California."

She took off into the air and the Hoove followed close behind. It was the first time in ninety-nine years that he was able to go wherever he wanted without restriction. The feeling of freedom was so thrilling that he whooped and hollered like a kid on a roller coaster.

They flew over mountain passes dotted with

clusters of glowing homes that looked out on the valleys below. They soared over the observatory with its giant telescope that looked out into the heavens. They swooped down into the zoo in Griffith Park to visit some of Anacapa's nocturnal animal friends, stopping first to pick eucalyptus leaves and bark to bring to the koalas. They crossed downtown, zigging and zagging among the now dark skyscrapers. They followed broad avenues lined with graceful palm trees. They passed neighbourhoods filled with schools and parks where the Hoove stopped to circle the bases in many of the local baseball diamonds. Finally, they arrived at the coast, circling the marina where sailboats bobbed in the harbour.

"This is quite a place," the Hoove said. "I can't believe what I've been missing all these years."

"And you haven't even seen the best part yet," Anacapa said. "Follow me."

She headed north from the marina, flying

low above the Santa Monica beaches. The Hoove looked out on the wide expanses of sand beneath him, and the ocean as it lapped up to the shore. He had never seen the ocean before, only read about it. It was more magnificent than he ever could have dreamed.

Before long, the navy blue night began to fade into the grey of early morning.

"I have an idea," the Hoove called out, flying up beside Anacapa. "Let's come in for a landing and watch the sun rise over the ocean."

Anacapa laughed.

"You have a lot to learn about nature," she said.

"What'd I say? The sun rises in the morning, right? How hard is that?"

"The sun rises in the east and sets in the west," she said. "This ocean is west. At the end of the day, you can come here to see the sunset, but if you want to see the sun rise, you have to look east."

"OK, you got me on a technicality," the Hoove

protested. "What I meant was that we should take a breather on the sand and watch the day break."

"I know just the spot," Anacapa said.

She swooped down from the sky and flew along the beach until she came to a long strand of rocks a safe distance away from where the waves were crashing.

"Let's sit on those rocks," she said. "It's my favourite place on this whole beach."

The Hoove followed her as she dived close to the waves and set herself down on the craggy rocks that looked out on the ocean. When he looked around, he realized that they were surrounded on three sides by the Pacific Ocean. In the distance, he could just see the outline of the Channel Islands. He sat there, listening to the waves lap on to the shore and taking it all in. Anacapa looked out at the Pacific, spread her arms wide, and said something in a language he didn't understand.

"Don't tell me," he said. "You're saying that

you're so glad to be here with your new best friend, Hoover Porterhouse the Third, pilot of the night skies and expert watcher of daybreak."

"This may be hard for you to understand," Anacapa answered, "but I actually was not talking about you."

"That's your first mistake."

Anacapa laughed. She was starting to understand the Hoove's sense of humour.

"Actually, I said the same thing I say every time I am here," she explained. "I asked the spirits of my ancestors to protect this beautiful sky and sea."

"You're pretty serious about this protection thing, aren't you?"

"Look around you, Hoover. Be silent. Appreciate where you are. And you will see why."

The Hoove sat there quietly next to Anacapa and watched the day emerge. At first, he was uncomfortable with the silence. He was used to filling the air with his words, with wisecracks, with swagger. But as the minutes ticked by, be became absorbed in what he was seeing and lost all need to talk.

He watched as the dark water turned blue in the morning sun. He saw the whitecaps appear and disappear with each wave. He heard the call of the seagulls as they circled above him. He examined the rock he was sitting on, and to his amazement, discovered a whole colony of living things in its tide pools. A sea urchin with spiny dark needles. A starfish missing a leg. A group of barnacles clinging to the rock and each other. A tiny hermit crab crawling on to a piece of kelp. Looking out to sea, he saw a pod of dolphins swim by, poking their grey heads in and out of the water playfully, squeaking in almost-human voices.

"Those guys aren't in danger too, are they?" he asked Anacapa.

"All marine life is in danger," she replied. "Our oceans have become a dumping ground for chemicals and plastic and other pollutants.

Unless we work to change that, everyone will be affected ... even those innocent dolphins out there."

The Hoove left her side and floated along the beach. In the light of day, he could see everything that was strewn about and left behind – water bottles, cigarette butts, pieces of fishing line, six-pack rings, even a child's broken orange plastic sand shovel. Without thinking about it, he set to work, gliding up and down the beach, picking up every piece of rubbish or plastic he could find. Within an hour, he had filled three rubbish bins with waste that he had collected.

Anacapa just watched him as he surveyed the beach, looking for every piece of litter or rubbish he could find. She knew what he was feeling – that when you care about something so much, protecting it doesn't seem like work. She floated over to him as he took a break and looked around.

"I didn't get all of it," he said, "but I made a dent. There's so much work to be done."

"Perhaps you can come back another day, Hoover."

"I wish," the Hoove said with genuine sadness. "But remember me, the idiot on a twenty-four-hour pass. I'd give anything to be able to help you with your mission. I love it here, and I never want to see it go away."

Suddenly, a huge grey-and-white seagull swopped down from the sky and landed on the rubbish bin right next to them. The bird cocked its head and stared at the Hoove, its beady eyes looking him up and down.

"What's with you?" the Hoove said to the bird. "Haven't you ever seen a ghost before?"

With a loud screech, the seagull let out a caw that could be heard up and down the beach. Then there was a flapping of wings, and within seconds, the bird was surrounded by a huge flock of gulls, hundreds of them beating the air with their wings and making a tremendous racket. In a mighty gust, they all flew up to the sky and into a formation.

"What's going on?" the Hoove said, covering his head.

"Look up!" Anacapa told him.

"Are you kidding? With all those birds overhead? No, thank you. I'm not in the mood to get pooped on."

"Just look, Hoover. Please."

The Hoove looked up in the sky, still shielding one eye with his hand. The birds had formed letters over the ocean, letters that covered the whole sky from one jetty to the next.

They spelled out *F–R–E–E–D–O–M*.

"Are you for real?" he called to the birds. "Did the Higher-Ups send you?"

The birds dispersed and with a thunderous fluttering of a million feathers, flew away. But before they disappeared completely, there was the sound of barking coming from the nearby jetty. The Hoove and Anacapa followed the sound and found a sea lion huddled under the rocks, barking. When it saw the Hoove, it spoke in a voice that was neither human nor sea lion.

"You have proven yourself," the sea lion croaked. "Now you are free. Do good work and be responsible for evermore."

That said, the sea lion dived into the ocean and swam away. It was the last Hoover Porterhouse ever saw of the Higher-Ups.

Chapter 13

"A sea lion?" Billy was saying, hopping up on his bed and bouncing up and down with excitement. "I don't believe it. You're kidding me, right?"

"I ask you, could I make up a story like that?" the Hoove answered, bouncing up and down along with Billy. "Before yesterday, I didn't even know what a sea lion was. I thought all lions lived in the jungle."

Billy and the Hoove were holed up in Billy's room, going over the events of the day. After getting his release from the Higher-Ups, the Hoove celebrated by taking Anacapa directly to Dodger Stadium.

"I wanted to go with you," he told Billy, "but I knew I couldn't spring you from baseball practice, and after waiting for ninety-nine years, I just couldn't wait another minute. But I brought you something."

He flew to his wardrobe and rummaged around, eventually emerging with half of a broken wooden baseball bat. He handed it to Billy.

"I found it behind the backstop," he said. "It's got to be game used. Tomorrow, I'll go back and look for the other half. When I find it, it's yours."

"Thanks, Hoove," Billy said, climbing down from the bed to inspect his new treasure. "I'll get my glue gun ready."

There was a knock on the door.

"Hey, Billy," Breeze yelled. "Ruby Baker's on the phone. She wants to know if you have her trophy."

"Tell her my mum brought it home and I'll bring it to her house later," Billy hollered back.

"I wish you could tell her yourself," Breeze shouted. "When are you going to learn to talk to girls?"

"Check back when I'm fourteen," Billy yelled.

When he heard Breeze's footsteps patter back down to her room, Billy knew it was safe to talk again.

"Turns out they gave trophies for last night's performances," he explained to the Hoove. "Ruby and I won for Most Unusual Performance in a Musical Number."

"Wait until I tell Anacapa," the Hoove said. "She'll be really proud of you."

They both laughed, and then fell silent as the reality of their new lives began to dawn on them.

"So I guess you'll be seeing Anacapa a lot now that you're free," Billy said at last.

"I promised I'd work on the beach clean-up with her. And we're going out to the Channel Islands to check on the brown pelican nesting sites. They're endangered, you know, so we have to protect their breeding area."

Billy nodded.

"You're going to be a busy guy," he said with more than a hint of sadness in his voice.

"Turns out being responsible is kind of a full-time job," the Hoove said. "Who knew?"

"Well, I'm glad that you and Anacapa are going to be such great friends," Billy said.

"Yeah. She's cool. But the one thing about her is that she doesn't get baseball. Not like you."

Billy nodded, and again, the two boys were silent.

"So I guess now that you have your freedom, you don't really need to live here any more . . . in my room, that is," Billy said at last.

Funny, he had been waiting for months for the day when he could have his room to himself, free from the Hoove's constant talking and interruptions and ghostly hubbub. Now that the day was here, though, he was feeling an unexpected lump in his throat.

"According to one very croaky sea lion, I'm free to live anywhere I want," the Hoove said, a little lump rising in his own throat.

"Oh," Billy said.

"Yeah," the Hoove nodded.

After another long silence, Billy finally got up the courage to ask.

"So what are you thinking, Hoove, now that you can pick anywhere to live? The locker room in Dodger Stadium? A fancy hotel overlooking the beach in Malibu? An orange grove in Riverside? Inside Space Mountain at Disneyland?"

"Those all sound pretty cool," the Hoove said. "But there's one thing they're all missing."

"Air conditioning?"

"No, you."

Billy looked up, surprised at the cracking sound in the Hoove's voice.

"So the thing is," the Hoove went on, swallowing the lump in his throat. "I've grown to like it here. You're the best friend a guy could have, for a human, that is. Your sassy sister is going to take some work, but your mum is the sweetest. And I've even developed a weird affection for Dr Dental Floss. The guy's got teeth filled with silver, but a heart of gold."

"So what are you saying, Hoove?" Billy asked, his heart beating a little faster than it had before. "That you want to continue living here? With me? In my room?"

"In *my* room," corrected the Hoove. "As long as you'll have me."

Billy literally jumped for joy and vaulted on to his bed. He started dancing around and around in a circle and making whooping noises. If only he could have danced that well at the Chumash night.

"This is so cool," he shouted. "The best of the best!"

The Hoove grabbed the broken Dodger bat and started beating out a rhythm on the wastebasket, chanting, "Billy! Billy! Billy!" Before long, Billy joined in, chanting "Hoove! Hoove! Hoove!"

The noise from Billy's room attracted a spectator. A boy in a one-horned buffalo mask tiptoed out of his house, crept up to Billy's window, and pressed his face against the glass.

Inside, he saw a broken bat dancing wildly in the air.

To him, it looked like weirdness was going on inside, but to Billy Broccoli and Hoover Porterhouse the Third, it was just another happy day at home.